My little sister.

Melissa folded her arms across her chest. "Stephanie invited me to her house. She's going to show me how to curl my hair."

"Sounds like a fun time," I muttered. Stephanie — playing Beauty Salon with *my* little sister?

"I can't wait!" Melissa declared. "I'm going to be so pretty, just like Stephanie."

What am I, chopped liver? I wanted to say. Now Melissa was not only dressing like Stephanie, she was also styling her hair the same way . . . what was next?

Look for these and other books
in the Sleepover Friends Series:

Big Sister Stephanie

Susan Saunders

AN
APPLE
PAPERBACK

SCHOLASTIC INC.
New York Toronto London Auckland Sydney

ISBN 0-590-43929-4

Copyright © 1990 by Daniel Weiss Associates, Inc. All rights reserved. Published by Scholastic Inc. APPLE PAPERBACKS is a registered trademark of Scholastic Inc. SLEEPOVER FRIENDS is a registered trademark of Daniel Weiss Associates, Inc.

12 11 10 9 8 7 6 5 4 3 2 1   0 1 2 3 4 5/9

Printed in the U.S.A.   28

First Scholastic printing, November 1990

Chapter
1

"So what do you think the movie should be about?" Lauren Hunter asked me.

"I think we should do 'The Life and Times of Stephanie Green.' " Stephanie leaned back on the bed and sighed. "Just think, I could be the next Marcy Monroe. I'll win Academy Awards, get to star with Kevin DeSpain, and move to Hollywood . . ." she said dreamily.

"It's only a home movie," I reminded her. I'm Kate Beekman.

"I didn't know you wanted to be an actress," Patti Jenkins said.

"Well, why not?" Stephanie said. "I mean, I have the right look."

Stephanie tends to get carried away with things. You know, like she believes in ghosts, and horoscopes, and astrology, and all that junk. She even

1

dresses dramatically — she almost always only wears clothes that are red, black, and white. I'm not really into clothes. I mean, of course I like to wear them, but jeans and sweatshirts are fine with me. And I don't have a color scheme yet or anything.

It was a Saturday morning after a sleepover at my house, and the four of us were sitting in my bedroom, trying to come up with an idea for a home movie. WRIV was sponsoring a competition for the best home movies. I figured I was a natural to win it. Of course there is only so much you can do with a camcorder.

"You wouldn't really move to Hollywood, would you?" Lauren asked with a worried look on her face.

"You'll have to ask my agent," Stephanie said in a snobby voice. Then she burst out laughing and Patti hit her over the head with one of my stuffed animals.

"Come on, you guys, get serious!" I said.

"Well, what are your ideas?" Stephanie replied.

"I was thinking we could do a story at school, showing what Riverhurst Elementary is like. Or, I could do a profile of each one of you, you know, with interviews and shots of you at home and school. I'd call it 'A Day in the Life of . . .'"

Patti frowned. "I don't know, Kate. I'm not so

sure I want everyone to see me on TV." She's kind of shy.

"Don't worry, I won't take any embarrassing shots," I promised her. "It'll be a serious film. I might show you with the science club, or . . ."

"Hey, Kate, do you have anything good to eat?" Lauren asked.

Sometimes Lauren is unbelievable! She's *always* hungry! "Why don't you go check the fridge?" I said. Lauren and I have been friends since we were really little, and she knows my house inside and out. My parents don't mind if she explores the refrigerator — they're used to it!

Lauren hopped up off the floor. "Anyone want anything?"

"Bring back lots of whatever you find," Stephanie instructed her, putting a tape into the cassette player. While she tried to teach Patti a new dance step, I thought about doing a movie of the four of us. It's strange that we're all such good friends because we're so different.

First, there's me. I'm short and I have straight blonde hair. I like movies . . . movies . . . and more movies! And Lauren always teases me for being really organized. I *do* like making lists, and jotting down ideas — they make it easier to get things done.

Lauren and I are complete opposites. The only

lists she probably makes are ones titled "Things Not to Do Today." Take her room, for example — it's always a total mess.

We don't look anything alike, either. She's tall and has brown hair and hazel eyes. And she likes jogging and other sports, which is something I can't really understand. Why run or jog somewhere when you can ride your bike or take the bus instead?

As I said, I've been friends with Lauren for a long time. We started having sleepovers at each other's house every Friday night when we were in first grade. Her father used to call us the Sleepover Twins. Now, with Stephanie and Patti, we're the four Sleepover Friends. (*Thought: Make a sleepover movie?* I jotted down in my notebook.)

Anyway, back to our differences. Patti's even taller than Lauren, and she likes sports, too. She's probably the nicest kid in our class — in the whole school — and one of the best students, too. She used to live in the city, just like Stephanie.

But that's the only thing they have in common! While Patti's shy, Stephanie is outgoing, and Stephanie would rather shop than study any day. Besides being particular about her clothes, her room is red, black, and white, too.

Lauren walked back into my room, balancing a bag of chips, a bunch of string cheese, and a plate of my homemade fudge.

4

Of course, a sleepover isn't a sleepover without great snacks — especially to Lauren, the Bottomless Pit. The really strange thing is how skinny she is, even though she eats all the time. I guess it's because she's so into sports.

"Why don't we do a monster movie — you know, like *Godzilla*, or *The Creature Who Ate Riverhurst*," Stephanie said.

"Starring Lauren, of course," I added with a grin.

Lauren put down the bag of chips. "Ha-ha," she said.

Just then the phone rang. I ran out and grabbed the extension in the hall, even though I was pretty sure the call wouldn't be for me. Most of my friends were right there in the room!

"Hello, Kate? This is Mrs. Green. Is Stephanie there?"

"Sure, hold on," I said. I handed the phone to Stephanie. "It's your mother."

Stephanie took the receiver from me with a puzzled look on her face. "Hi, Mom, what's up?" she said. As she listened to her mother, the expression on Stephanie's face changed into a frown. "Uh-huh," she said, rolling her eyes at us. "Okay. Bye." She hung up the phone with an irritated sigh. "Well, there goes *my* Saturday."

"What do you mean?" Patti asked. "Is something wrong?"

5

"No more than usual," Stephanie replied, picking up a piece of fudge. "I have to go home and help my mom take the twins to the doctor. It's time for their six-month checkup."

Stephanie has a twin sister and brother, Emma and Jeremy. She's always trying to get her mom to dress them in red, black, and white instead of pink and blue. Anyway, unlike when she was an only child, now Stephanie has more and more household responsibilities — like taking care of the twins.

"Want me to come with you?" Patti offered.

Stephanie shook her head. "No, that's okay. It's going to be pretty boring."

"I can't wait to see the twins again," Lauren said enthusiastically. "They're so cute. Have they grown much since the last time I was at your house?"

Stephanie shrugged. "Since last week? Nope. They can't stand up yet. They can't even crawl."

Just then, *my* little sister Melissa ran down the hallway, screaming something to her best friend, Eileen.

I put my hands over my ears. "You should be glad they can't do anything!" I said. "I'm living with the loudest person on earth."

My little sister can be such a pain! I tell my parents about it, but they say I just have to be patient with her.

"That's what we can do!" Lauren announced.

"A horror movie, featuring Melissa the Monster!"

"It would be rated 'O' — for Obnoxious!" I said.

"Come on, she's not that bad," Patti said. "Is she?" Patti has a little brother, Horace, who's two years younger than Melissa. Compared to Melissa, Horace is an absolute angel. Then again, so am I!

"Yesterday she brought my big book on horses to school to show all her friends," I said.

"What's so horrible about that?" Stephanie asked.

"Well, one of her friends ripped one of the pages out." I was really mad, because I'd gotten it for a birthday present. "It's ruined!" I said.

"Well, it *is* only one page," Patti said.

I shook my head. "She's always ruining my stuff. I'm going to have to lock up the video camera so she doesn't mess that up, too!" (*Note: Ask Dad about getting a safe,* I wrote in my notebook.) "She'll probably break it or erase all the film."

Stephanie stood up and brushed the crumbs off her pants. "I guess I should get going," she said glumly. "Did I tell you what happened the last time I tried to give Jeremy a bottle?" She wrinkled her nose. "Yuck! When I tried to burp him, he spit up! And on my new red sweater with the white triangles on it, too!"

I laughed. Stephanie was definitely not the baby-sitter type. She always had that "I'd Rather Be Shopping" look on her face whenever she held one of the twins.

"I don't think it's very funny," Stephanie said, glaring at me. "I'm going to be stuck at home all weekend, probably."

"Cheer up, Stephanie — you could be stuck inside with Melissa," I told her. "At least Emma and Jeremy don't try to *do* anything to you!"

"That's just it," Stephanie complained. "They don't do anything! They were fine for a couple of months, when they started sleeping through the whole night. But now they're teething and it seems like all they do is cry."

"Think of it this way, Stephanie — it's good experience," said Lauren. "Pretty soon you'll be able to start a professional baby-sitting service."

"I don't think I want to," Stephanie admitted. "I'm not very good at it."

"You'll get used to it," Patti predicted. "If I can, then anybody can!"

Stephanie wrapped her scarf around her neck. "Will you guys promise to call me so I don't go crazy?"

"Of course, we will," Lauren said. "And once we figure out the movie, we'll let you know what it's going to be — right, Kate?"

"Right. We'll even let you choose your part," I

told her. I had gotten into trouble with everyone a while ago when we were doing a float for the Riverhurst School Homecoming parade. I guess I was trying to do everything my own way without listening to their ideas. Anyway, Stephanie had hated her part on the float, and I didn't want to go through that again.

"Okay, see you later," Stephanie mumbled, opening the door.

"Good luck," I said with a smile.

Melissa and Eileen ran down the hall shrieking again and practically plowed right into Stephanie. Maybe a horror movie wasn't such a bad idea after all, I thought. Something about an eight-year-old.

Chapter 2

"Ugh!" I put down my fork. "I'm bringing my lunch from now on." It was Monday, and the four of us were sitting in the school cafeteria at our usual table.

"This is definitely the worst thing they've ever served," Patti agreed. "At least the desserts are good." She took a bite of chocolate cake.

"I'm going to start a petition," I said. "No more sloppy joes."

Lauren laughed. "Nice sweater, Patti," she said. Patti was wearing a green sweater that had little buttons at the neckline. It brought out the color of her eyes.

"Thanks," Patti said.

"Where did you get it?" I asked her.

"At Just Juniors on Saturday," she said. "I went with my mom after I left your house."

"At least your mom still does stuff with you," Stephanie grumbled.

"What are you talking about?" Lauren said.

"My parents don't even know I'm alive," Stephanie said, mashing her piece of cake with her fork. "The only time they want to see me is when they need me to do something for them — like baby-sit, or do the dishes." She shook her head.

"It won't always be like that," Patti said. "When Horace was born, it seemed like my parents spent all of their time with him. I always had to be quiet so I wouldn't wake him up."

"I hate that!" Stephanie chimed in. "I can't ever play my radio or watch TV in my room when they're sleeping. And they're *always* sleeping."

"They'll grow out of it soon," Patti said, "and everything will go back to normal."

Stephanie shook her head. "It'll never be normal — not with twins. Everyone makes such a big deal about them all the time."

"Well, it'll be fun having a little sister and brother when they're older," I commented.

"Look who's talking! You're the one who can't stand having a little sister," Stephanie said.

I shrugged my shoulders. "With any luck, Emma and Jeremy won't turn out like Melissa. Look at it this way — when they're older, they'll be able to play together and you won't have to entertain them."

"It must be weird, having someone younger around the house," Lauren said. Her brother, Roger, is seventeen. "I wonder if there were ever times when Roger didn't want me around?"

"Sure there were—remember the time he locked us in your room? And he was always trying to scare us with creepy stories and slimy bugs and stuff so we'd get lost," I reminded her.

"You're right. Well, at least he grew out of it." Lauren took a sip of milk.

"The point is, Stephanie, this is just a phase," Patti said. "Pretty soon your parents won't need you to help out so much. Trust me."

"Maybe I'll move out to the apartment," Stephanie said, referring to the playhouse in her backyard. "That way I'll be able to listen to music whenever I want."

After school we went to my house to start working on my — I mean, *our* — movie. We had decided to go with "A Day in the Life of a Fifth-Grader." Only we weren't going to put in all the boring things about fifth grade, like how you have to get up early in the morning, and who you have to sit behind in class, and what the teacher thinks of your book reports. We just wanted to show the fun stuff.

The first thing we had to do was make a few signs to put at the beginning of the movie, with the title and our names. Stephanie was in charge of the art for the signs. She's really good at drawing and painting.

"Oops," Stephanie suddenly said. "I need another poster board. I messed this one up. Lauren, can you help me?" she asked. She picked up another piece of poster board from the floor and hauled it over to my dad's worktable. We were working in the basement. There's a lot of room down there and we can't mess anything up because the only stuff that's down there is junk.

The door to the basement opened and I heard someone clomp down the stairs.

"Melissa, what are *you* doing down here?" I demanded. "I told you this was off-limits."

"What are you guys doing?" she asked. She wandered over to Stephanie and Lauren.

"Don't bother them," I warned her. "They're working on something very important."

Melissa leaned forward as far as she could without falling over, trying to get a look at the poster. "What are you doing?" she asked Lauren.

"We're just making a sign," Lauren told her quickly. She handed Stephanie another Magic Marker.

"What's it for?" Melissa went on.

I put my hands on her shoulders and turned her around. "None of your business," I said. "Why don't you go upstairs and read a book or something?" I tried to push her toward the stairs.

"Cut it out!" she complained.

"Melissa, I told you, what we're doing is important and we can't be disturbed."

She gave me this really pathetic, sad look, but I wasn't about to fall for it. She uses it all the time to get herself out of trouble with Mom and Dad. "Quit pouting and go to your room," I told her.

She pouted for another minute, then took off and bolted up the stairs. I hoped she wasn't going to complain to my mom. I don't see why I should get in trouble for *her* being a pain.

"We'll have to use that in the movie," Lauren said.

I looked at her, confused. "Use what?"

"Being a fifth-grader means being harassed by your little sister," she answered.

"Not if I can help it," I muttered to myself. "How's the sign going?" I asked Stephanie.

"Fine," she said. "I finished the letters, now all I have to do is draw some designs around the outside."

"Did you do the credits yet?" I couldn't wait to see how "Directed by Kate Beekman" was going to look.

Stephanie shook her head. "Don't you think we

14

should put those at the end? We might not know who's going to be in this until we're finished."

"That's true," Patti agreed.

I shook my head. "No, they have to go at the beginning! That's the way it's done."

"Let's make up stage names for ourselves!" Stephanie said eagerly. "That's what all the famous actors do. They change their names when they move to Hollywood so they'll sound like movie stars."

"How about Patti Joujen?" Lauren said with a phony French accent.

Patti burst out laughing. "And you'll just go by your first name — Lauren."

I threw up my hands. "Come on, you guys — we have work to do!"

Just then the door at the top of the stairs opened again and I heard a familiar footstep.

"Melissa . . ." I said slowly.

She held up a bunch of Magic Markers. "I brought some stuff to help."

"You can't help," I told her.

She gave me that pitiful look again. "Why not?" she pleaded.

"Because this a very special project. And it's for fifth-graders — not third-graders," I said.

"I have special colors," she said, holding up the Magic Markers again.

"Let's see," Stephanie said sweetly.

My eyes practically popped out of my head. "Don't encourage her," I whispered to Stephanie.

"We could use a few more colors," she admitted.

"I have purple!" Melissa announced. She pulled the cap off one of the markers and headed for the poster board.

"No!" I grabbed her arm. "We don't need your kind of help. Get lost!" I was feeling so frustrated — why couldn't she leave me and my friends alone for once?

Melissa whirled around and ran up the stairs. "I hate you!" she yelled. Then she slammed the door as hard as she could.

"Remind me to buy a lock for that door," I said.

"She just wanted to help," Stephanie said, making some squiggles around the title.

"Help ruin everything," I reminded her.

"Whatever. I'm kind of thirsty. Does anyone else want something to drink?" Stephanie headed for the stairs.

Lauren and Patti both nodded. "Bring down four Dr Peppers," I said.

"Okay — be right back!" She bounded up the stairs and into the kitchen.

She came back a few minutes later with the sodas. "I saw Melissa upstairs," she said.

"So what?" I asked.

"So, she was watching TV, and she looked really sad. Don't you think she was kind of upset about not being able to help us?" Stephanie asked me.

"You *were* kind of rough on her," Patti said.

"Am I hearing things? Do you guys actually think I should be *nice* to Melissa?"

"Maybe there is something she could help us do," Stephanie suggested.

I shook my head. "Don't you remember what happened the last time we let her in on one of our projects? When we were making a cake for the bake sale at school, and we told her she could help by greasing the pans — and she forgot? The cake came out of the pan in about a million pieces!"

Stephanie grinned. "That's right — I forgot."

Lauren started laughing. "And we decided we'd just have to eat all the pieces and start over!"

"No, *you* decided that," I teased her.

"I guess you're right, Kate," Stephanie agreed.

I set down my can of soda and rubbed my hands together. "Okay, break's over — let's get back to work."

"Yes, master," Lauren answered, bowing.

We filmed the title and the "Directed by" sign and then mapped out what to do during the rest of the week. We decided to play it by ear — I'd take the camera to school one day and get some candid shots of kids in our class. Other than that, I would just try to catch everyone doing things they would normally do. I was looking forward to it.

When it was time for everyone to go home for dinner, we headed upstairs.

"I wish we could just order a pizza and stay here," Stephanie said, peering out the window.

"I know — it's been freezing cold lately," Lauren added. "But at least you live nearby. I'll have to take the bus all the way over to Brio Drive."

Lauren and I had grown up living practically next door to each other on Pine Street, but recently her family had moved across town. I hate it. We don't see each other as much anymore, and I can't just run over whenever I feel like it.

"Maybe my parents can give you a ride," I said. "Hold on." I found my father in the den. He was watching TV with Melissa. "Dad, can you do me a big favor, and give Lauren a ride home? It's practically dark out and it's so cold."

He stood up. "Sure — just let me get my coat."

"Thanks!" I told him. Then I ran back to the living room. Everyone was busy putting on their jackets and bundling up to go outside.

Stephanie put on her scarf, hat, and mittens. "Time to face the Arctic," she joked, opening the

18

door just wide enough to slip out. "See you guys later! Bye, Melissa!"

I shook my head as I watched Stephanie run down the sidewalk. Maybe the cold had affected her brain. She was acting as if she *cared* about Melissa!

Chapter 3

"I feel like an idiot," Lauren said. She was trying to smile and look into the camera while she built a snowman.

"Just a few more seconds," I told her. "There!"

"I'm not sure about this outdoor shot idea." Stephanie rubbed her arms. "I think a day in the life of a fifth-grader in the winter should be pretty much indoors. I mean, that's where I spend the winter."

"In a nice warm kitchen," Lauren said dreamily.

Patti shivered. "Better yet, in front of the fire-place!"

Sometimes it's hard having wimps for friends. "It's not that cold," I said. Then I looked around the park to see what else would make a good shot for the movie. There had been a huge snowstorm the night before, and the park was full of kids playing, having snowball fights, and sliding. A bunch of sixth-graders were sledding down the big hill. I spotted Taylor Sprouse right away. He's the only kid in our school who has a black winter jacket, a black scarf, and black winter boots. Stephanie has a crush on him — I used to, too, but I got tired of Taylor's attitude . . . and his clothes. Talk about boring!

"Stephanie, look," I said, hoping it would cheer her up. She still seemed down in the dumps. "Taylor's over there with his friends."

She shaded her eyes with her hand and gazed over at the hill. "You're right. How about if we casually stroll over and take some pictures of him? We'll sneak up on them — they'll never know," Stephanie assured me. She started walking over to the hill. "Come on!"

I wasn't too thrilled about putting Taylor in the movie. He's the most conceited boy I've ever seen. He's always combing his hair, and he walks around like he owns the planet!

But I trudged after Stephanie anyway, along with Patti and Lauren. When Stephanie makes up her mind, she doesn't give up.

"I guess you're not cold anymore, Stephanie," Lauren said.

Patti giggled.

Stephanie blushed. "Cut it out," she whispered

as we got closer. We hid behind a row of trees along the side of the hill and waited for Taylor to come down.

"Here they come," Stephanie whispered. About eight boys were crowded onto one toboggan, and they were hurtling down the hill at top speed. "Look at them go!"

I turned the camera on, but I didn't point it at the toboggan. Instead, I recorded Stephanie's face as she watched them fly past us. She looked like one of those girls you see at rock concerts, as if she were going to die from the excitement of being so close to Taylor. I decided I'd change the title of the movie to "A Day in the Life of a Boy-Crazy Fifth-Grader."

"Did you get that?" she asked. The boys were at the bottom of the hill and had started to walk back up.

"Uh . . . sure," I said.

Stephanie gave me a suspicious look. "Could you really see him or were the trees in the way?"

"Actually, I didn't quite get a good shot," I admitted.

"Well, you'd better take another then," Stephanie said, "just to make sure." She grinned at me. "This is one movie I won't mind watching with you!"

We waited until the boys were all set for another run down the hill. Then, just as Taylor pushed off and jumped onto the back of the toboggan, I stepped out from behind the trees and started filming them.

Halfway down the steep hill, they hit a big bump — and Taylor went flying off the back of the toboggan. It was hysterical! He landed facedown in the snow. We all burst out laughing — even Stephanie.

When Taylor stood up, he was covered with snow. Instead of wearing all black, he was wearing all white!

"I hope you're getting this, Kate," Lauren gasped between laughs.

"I wouldn't miss it for the world!" I used the zoom feature and got a great close-up of Taylor. He was scowling as he brushed the snow off his face.

"Don't you think he looks good in white?" Stephanie commented.

"He looks like the abominable snowman!" Patti added. She was laughing so hard she was holding her stomach. It was great to see the "perfect" Taylor Sprouse looking like an idiot for once. His hair was *seriously* out of place.

Taylor glared in our direction. I turned off the camera and put it behind my back. "Let's go before he catches us," I said.

"Let's go over to the skating rink," Lauren suggested.

We walked down the hill toward the skating area. You can skate there for free and they light it up at night and everything.

"Why don't you guys skate, and I'll watch," I said.

"Well . . . okay." Patti shrugged. "What have I got to lose?"

"What about you, Stephanie?" Lauren asked. "You're the best of any of us."

Stephanie looked glumly at her watch. "I have to go home. It's Tuesday, remember?" Stephanie baby-sits for the twins every Tuesday and Thursday afternoon. "In fact, I should have been there ten minutes ago — my dad's going to be furious. Today I'm supposed to start dinner while *he* watches the twins."

"Speaking of the twins," I said, "I want to use them in the movie. I think they'll look great on film! Babies always do."

Stephanie stared at me. "Oh, sure," she said. "Why don't you make them the stars of the movie, too? My parents will probably offer to buy it from you!"

I knew Stephanie didn't like having to baby-sit, but I hadn't realized she was still having so much trouble adjusting to them — until now!

"Stephanie, there're going to be lots of shots of you in the movie!" I told her. "Don't worry about

24

that. We'll shoot more skating scenes tomorrow, if you want," I said.

"Yeah, I have to get going soon anyway," Patti added as she laced up her skates.

"We'll just practice today, and then do the real thing tomorrow," Lauren said.

Stephanie let out a loud sigh as she hoisted her schoolbag over her shoulder. "Maybe I'll stay and watch for a few minutes," she said.

Patti and Lauren headed out onto the ice. Lauren skated around the edge of the rink, trying to go fast. Patti was trying a few moves. She did a figure eight and then she started skating backwards. Before she knew what was happening, she plowed into a kid who looked like he was about fifteen — and they both fell down. I couldn't resist using the zoom to get a close-up of Patti — I knew she'd be blushing like crazy!

Just then, something wet and cold hit me from behind — a snowball, right on the neck! I was so startled I dropped the camcorder.

I spun around, and saw Melissa. She was giggling and pointing at me. "I hit Kate!" she cried. "I got Kate!"

"And I'll get you!" I said under my breath. The camera could have been ruined! Luckily for me, it hadn't landed on the ice — it had landed in a snowbank on the edge of the rink. I picked it up and tested all the buttons. It still worked. I opened my jacket and used my sweater to rub all the snow off of it.

"Why do you always have to spoil everything?" I asked Melissa. "I had a perfect shot of Patti, and now it's probably ruined."

Stephanie was actually giggling. "You have to admit, the kid has good aim," she said.

Melissa was still standing there, grinning at me. "I got Kate!" she said again.

"Yeah, and you almost broke my camera!" I told her. "Wait until I tell Mom and Dad about this!"

Melissa's smile vanished. "I'm sorry," she said softly.

I wasn't about to forgive her. "You should be sorry. You messed up the whole movie," I said. I turned to Patti, Lauren, and Stephanie. "See, I told you she would ruin it."

"I didn't ruin it!" Melissa cried. Then she turned and ran across the field, toward our house.

"She didn't mean to make you drop the camera, you know," Stephanie said a few seconds later.

"How do you know?" I said angrily. "You're not exactly an expert on little kids!"

When I saw the sad, shocked look on Stephanie's face, I wanted to take back everything I'd said. I hadn't meant to be so mean. It's just that Melissa gets to me sometimes!

"I'm sorry, Stephanie," I said. "I didn't mean that."

She just looked at the ground and muttered, "I have to go home. My dad's waiting for me." Then she turned and ran off in the same direction as Melissa.

As we watched her go, Patti said, "I hope she gets used to being an older sister soon. She's miserable!"

"No kidding," added Lauren. "All I know is, I'd hate to have to baby-sit all the time — and I like kids!"

"She'll get over it," I said with a shrug.

Patti and Lauren looked at me as if I had said the wrong thing. "What?" I asked.

"Well, you could be a little more understanding about it," said Patti. "She's having a really hard time."

I wiped some more of the wet snow out of my jacket collar. "So am I!" I said.

Chapter 4

I got the bad news at breakfast the next morning. We were having a half day at school because of some teachers meeting, and I'd planned to spend the afternoon with my friends. But my mother announced that it was time for our yearly winter shopping trip — you know, new coats, boots, turtlenecks, the works.

The bad news was that Melissa was coming along.

I hadn't spoken to her since the snowball incident, and I didn't want to. I tried to convince my mom that I didn't need any new clothes. I hadn't grown that much since last year, and my jacket still fit.

"Kate, it's all frayed around the bottom and you lost the hood, remember?" she said. "I'm sure you'd rather have a new jacket. And I know you need some new boots."

That was true — I'd been wearing my sneakers so far that winter, and they weren't very warm. "Why don't you just give me the money, and I'll go to the mall with Lauren on Saturday?" I suggested.

She shook her head. "I want to be there to help you decide which things to get. I'll pick you up at school, okay? No more arguments."

I stood up from the kitchen table and let out a big sigh. "All right." Then I put on my jacket — it did look kind of ratty, now that she mentioned it — and picked up my schoolbag. "See you later," I said.

As I walked down our sidewalk, I thought about the last time we had gone on one of our family shopping trips, when Melissa had tried to convince my parents to buy her everything at Playing Around, a huge toy store. Then she ran off to talk to one of her friends and ended up getting lost. We had to page her over the mall's loudspeaker system. It was really embarrassing!

"Hi, Kate!" Patti greeted me. On days like today, when it's not too cold, we meet and ride our bikes to school.

"Hi," I mumbled.

"What's wrong?" Lauren asked. "You sound so bummed! Don't forget, it's a half day at school — we get out at noon!" she said excitedly.

I groaned. "That's what's bothering me."

She stared at me. "Don't tell me you *want* to spend the afternoon learning about the life cycle of a plant."

I shook my head. "No, it's not that. I have to spend the afternoon at the mall — "

"What's so bad about that?" Stephanie interrupted.

" — with my mother and Melissa," I finished. I turned to her and raised one eyebrow. "Now do you see why I'm dreading it?"

She shifted her knapsack to her other shoulder. "Well, of course it would be a lot more fun if it were the four of us. But the mall's the mall. Do you think your mom would mind if we came along?"

"What a great idea!" I said. "My mom said she didn't want me to go with just you guys, but she didn't say you guys couldn't come along!" I turned to Lauren. "How about it?"

She shook her head. "I can't. Roger and I have to take Bullwinkle to the vet." Bullwinkle is the Hunters' dog, and he's huge. It takes at least two people to deal with him on a car trip. He's always trying to jump onto the driver.

"I can't go, either," Patti said. "I have to work on a new Quarks project." The Quarks is the name of a science club at school.

"Well, I can definitely go," Stephanie said. "I don't have anything to do this afternoon, really."

30

"Are you sure you want to?" I was amazed. I couldn't understand why anyone not related to Melissa would want to subject herself to the torture of spending time with her.

"There are a few things I want to check out at the mall," Stephanie said. "And for once I don't have to go home and change diapers!"

When she put it that way, going to the mall did look a lot more attractive. "Okay — I'll call my mom at recess and ask her if you can come," I said. If Stephanie joined us, Melissa and my mom could go off and look at kids' stuff while Stephanie helped me pick out a new jacket. "Thanks for saving me, Stephanie," I said.

"From what?" she asked me.

"From the monster!" I said, and we both laughed.

"Here, Melissa, try this one on." Stephanie pulled a jacket off the hanger and held it out to her. "Isn't it cute?"

Melissa slipped the jacket on and zipped it up. She ran over and stood in front of the mirror. "It's ugly," she said, frowning at her reflection.

I let out a loud sigh. My mother was off looking at some clothes for herself, and she had stranded us with Melissa in the children's section of Grand's.

Stephanie flipped through the other jackets and

took another one off the rack. "What about this?" The jacket she was holding out was red, with white cuffs and a black hood.

Melissa stared at it, and then at Stephanie, who was wearing her red, black, and white jacket, a white scarf, and black mittens. "Okay!" she agreed.

Stephanie followed her over to the mirror and helped her try on the jacket. When she and Melissa stood next to each other, I laughed out loud. They were dressed almost exactly alike!

"What's so funny?" Stephanie asked me.

"Oh, nothing," I told her, shaking my head.

Just then my mom walked over. "How's it going, girls?" she asked. She adjusted the hood on Melissa's jacket and patted the sleeves a few times. "Do you like this one, honey?"

Melissa nodded eagerly. "I have to have it."

Mom looked at the price tag. "Okay! That was easy," she said, smiling at Stephanie. "What about you, Kate? Have you found anything?"

"Not yet," I said.

"Well, I'm going to look at a few more things in the ladies' department. Come find me when you need me," she said. She headed back to the other side of the store.

"Here," I said to Melissa, "put your old jacket back on, and carry the new one."

She shook her head. "I'm never taking this off —

I love it!'' She ran over and admired herself in the mirror again.

Stephanie said, ''Melissa, don't you want to get some boots to go with your jacket?''

Melissa turned around and beamed. ''Yes!'' She skipped over to Stephanie. ''Let's go look at the boots.''

''Wait a minute — *I* have to find a jacket first,'' I said.

''Oh, you don't want to get it here,'' Stephanie said with a wave of her hand. ''We'll go to Good Sports — they have a great selection of ski jackets.''

I frowned at her. ''I'm not exactly a skier. I'll look stupid in one of those neon jackets.''

''They have other colors, too,'' Stephanie said. ''That's where I got *my* jacket!''

I looked at her and Melissa in their almost-identical jackets and shook my head. Three white, red, and black jackets was too much!

Melissa was tugging at my sleeve. ''Come *on*, Kate,'' she urged me. ''I have to get my boots.''

''Okay, okay!'' I said. She took off running for the shoe department.

A few minutes later, Melissa had a pair of — what else — black boots on.

''See, they go perfectly with the jacket,'' Stephanie explained. ''Like my boots! It's important to make sure your clothes go together,'' Stephanie went on. "That way, you always have something to wear — because everything matches! And red, black, and white are the best colors because they really stand out. People notice you."

"Melissa, are you sure you don't want to try some others on?" I asked her. "You usually get blue boots."

"Blue won't go with her jacket," Stephanie said, shaking her head.

I felt like we were outfitting Melissa for a beauty pageant or something! Usually she just wore whatever she had.

"Next, you should get a scarf to match the jacket and the boots," Stephanie continued. "And then — "

"I think I'll go find my mom," I interrupted. I didn't feel like listening to the rest of the fashion seminar.

On the way to the ladies' department, I stopped in the juniors section to look at jackets. I found one I really liked — it was navy blue with green cuffs and a green collar. And it was on sale, so I knew my mom would like it, too.

I found my mom and brought her over to the shoe department first so she could take a look at Melissa's boots. "Oh, those are darling!" she said. "Very nice with the jacket." Melissa grinned happily as my mother paid for the jacket and the boots.

"Let's look at your jacket now," Mom said to me.

"Oh, did you find one?" Stephanie asked.

I nodded. "In juniors." We headed over to the rack and I put it on. "What do you think?" I said, zipping it all the way up to the collar.

Stephanie wrinkled her nose. "It's okay."

"Just okay?" I asked her. I took a look at myself in the mirror. "I think it's really nice."

"It doesn't match your boots," Melissa said, giving me a disapproving look.

Give me a break! I thought.

"Is it warm enough?" my mother asked.

"Sure," I said. "Aren't these cuffs cool?" I asked Stephanie. They were made out of a special shiny material.

She felt them, and shrugged. "Are you sure you don't want to look in the ski store?"

"It *is* the first one you've tried on," my mother said. "If you want to look around a little, that's fine."

"No," I said firmly. "I'll take it." I slipped out of the jacket and handed it to my mother. So what if Stephanie didn't approve — she didn't like anything blue or green. They were my favorite colors. And they used to be Melissa's, too!

"Do you two want to take off and do some shopping on our own?" my mother asked me and

Stephanie. "I can take Melissa to Playing Around if you want to go to the music store or get a soda or something."

I started to say, "Yes!" but before I could, Stephanie said, "No, that's okay — we still have some things to look at."

We? Who's *we?* I wanted to say. Stephanie and Melissa?

Stephanie and Melissa started walking back to the children's section. As I trailed after them, I heard Stephanie saying, "Now, after you get the scarf, we can look at some socks. Socks *really* make an outfit complete."

I let out a loud sigh. It looked like I was going to be living with an eight-year-old clotheshorse from now on.

Chapter
5

I practically choked on my cornflakes the next morning when Melissa came down to breakfast. She was wearing black jeans, a white shirt, and a red sweater. Just like Stephanie!

Melissa pranced over to the table and sat down opposite me.

"Hey, Melissa," I said, "I have a joke for you. What's black and white and read all over?"

She poured some milk into her bowl and sloshed the cereal around. "I don't know." She shrugged. "Me?"

"No — a newspaper! Get it?"

She just kept chewing her cereal.

Little kids — what do they know? I thought to myself. At least I could understand jokes when *I* was eight. "Don't you get it?" I asked Melissa.

Melissa looked confused. "Mom, can I go over

to Stephanie's house after school?" she suddenly said.

This time I was lucky I wasn't eating anything, because I definitely would have choked! "Does Stephanie know anything about this?" I asked Melissa. "Or are you just planning to show up there?"

Melissa folded her arms across her chest. "She invited me," she said.

"Is that true, honey?" my mother asked her.

Melissa nodded. "She's going to show me how to curl my hair."

My mother looked as surprised as I felt. "Well, isn't that nice of her," she said. "I suppose you can go. But be careful — curling irons are very hot, you know."

"She's going to do it for me!" Melissa announced happily. "I don't have to do anything."

"Sounds like a fun time," I muttered. Stephanie — playing Beauty Salon with *my* little sister? "Are you sure she didn't just say that you should get it curled some time?" I asked Melissa.

"Nope! She's going to pick me up at my classroom," Melissa declared. "I can't wait! I'm going to be so pretty, just like Stephanie."

What am I, chopped liver? I wanted to say. Which reminded me — I had to give my cat, Fredericka, breakfast. Great, I thought, opening a can of cat food and scraping it into her dish. Now Melissa was not only dressing like Stephanie, she was also styling her hair the same way. . . . What was next?

My mom gave us a ride to school that morning because it was snowy. When I got to my class, I headed straight for Stephanie's desk. I don't believe in beating around the bush.

"Stephanie, is it true you're meeting Melissa after school to do her hair?" I asked.

Stephanie shrugged her shoulders. "She said she liked my hair and wished she could have hair like it. So I told her I'd show her how she could make hers curly."

"What are you guys talking about?" Patti asked, coming over to us.

"Stephanie's going to give Melissa a make-over this afternoon," I said. "She's going to transform her from a monster into . . . a curly-headed monster!"

"She's not a monster," Stephanie said.

I stared at Stephanie. "You don't live with Melissa," I reminded her.

"I know, but I just thought it would be fun for her to fool around with hair and clothes and stuff like that," Stephanie said.

"I bet she'll enjoy it," Patti said with a polite smile.

"Maybe she will," I admitted, "but don't blame me if she tears all your hair out!"

Then the bell rang and we sat down in our seats. Lauren ran in at the last second. We sit next to each other, and I had to let her know what was happening with Melissa and her new buddy, Stephanie. While Mrs. Mead passed out corrected homework assignments, I scribbled this note:

Steph is acting weird. Today she's meeting Melissa after school to curl Melissa's hair. What is going on?

"What is the deal?" I asked everyone at the end of the day as we watched Stephanie walk off to Melissa's classroom to pick her up.

"I think it's kind of nice that she's doing something with Melissa this afternoon," Patti commented.

"It just doesn't make sense," I said. "You guys don't know what happened yesterday at the mall." I told them how Stephanie had convinced Melissa that red, black, and white were the only colors for her, and how she had spent every minute with Melissa when we could have run off to get ice cream or look at tapes by ourselves.

"So now Melissa's dressing the same way?" Lauren asked.

I nodded. "Isn't that weird?"

"It is," agreed Patti. "I mean, it sure doesn't

sound like Stephanie. She has to baby-sit this afternoon, right?" She was right — it was Thursday. "So now she's going to have to worry about Emma, Jeremy, and Melissa. She's really going to have her hands full!"

"I don't know what's going on," I said, "but if you ask me, Stephanie's going crazy. Can you imagine wanting to spend an afternoon with Melissa?" I shuddered. "I'd rather do my homework!"

Later that afternoon, I was helping my mom cut up some vegetables for salad when Melissa barged through the door. "Look at my hair!" she cried.

I turned around from the sink. Melissa was dancing in little circles around the kitchen, swinging her head from side to side.

"Isn't it pretty?" she went on.

"It looks very nice," my mother said. Melissa danced up to her and Mom touched her hair. "It's so soft! I think you look beautiful."

Melissa sashayed over to me. "Mom says I'm beautiful!"

I reached out and pulled on one of her curls. It sprang back into shape. "Stephanie did a good job," I said. Fair is fair.

"I'm going to wear my hair like this every day!" Melissa proclaimed, doing a little hop around the room. I could tell she was only jumping around so much because she wanted to feel her curls bouncing on her shoulders.

"I'm not so sure about that," my mother said with a smile. "Unless you can get Stephanie to come over here and do it for you every morning."

"Don't even say it!" I said under my breath, turning back to the carrot I was peeling.

"I hope you thanked Stephanie," my mother said to Melissa. "She went to a lot of trouble, you know."

"I did," Melissa said proudly. "Three times!" Then she ran into the living room and turned on the TV.

"That was very thoughtful of Stephanie," Mom said. "Don't you think so, Kate?"

Actually, I thought it was very *weird*, but I didn't tell my mother that. Instead, I just nodded.

"She's really very sweet," my mother continued.

Suddenly my house had turned into the headquarters for the Stephanie Green Fan Club! I couldn't believe it! I quickly chopped up the carrot and tossed it into the salad. "Mom, can I go upstairs now?" I asked.

"Sure, I'll finish up here," she said.

I took the stairs two at a time and when I got to my room, I almost slammed the door. I didn't know why, but I was really bothered by the way Stephanie was acting. Melissa thought Stephanie was the greatest thing since peanut-butter-and-jelly, and now it seemed like my mom did, too! Melissa had never acted that way toward *me* before.

I picked up a sweater from the bed and folded it neatly. I hate it when clothes are lying around my room. I reached up and tried to put the sweater onto its stack. Suddenly, all the sweaters came toppling down and fell on top of my head. What a rotten day! Now I had to fold and stack each one of them again. It was all Melissa's fault, too. If she hadn't made me so mad, I would have been more careful.

I thought about it for a minute. Melissa hadn't done anything wrong, really. I mean, she hadn't done anything to mess up my life, for once. She'd actually stayed out of my way all afternoon.

Maybe she wasn't just an annoying eight-year-old. If Stephanie could stand an afternoon with her, then I probably could, too.

I placed the last sweater on the stack and smoothed the top of it. Was it possible that I had been treating Melissa unfairly? I hadn't given her much of a chance lately. Maybe she was growing up. It was hard to believe, but maybe it was true.

But that still didn't explain why Stephanie wanted to be Melissa's best friend.

I decided to call Lauren and see if she had any ideas. I went out into the hall and picked up the extension.

"Is this the famous actress Lauren?" I said in a phony foreign accent when she answered the phone.

"Yes, it is," she said. "No autographs, please."

"I'm just calling to let you know that I have a junior starlet living in my house," I said. "She's a Shirley Temple type — curly blonde hair, dances around a lot. . . ."

"You mean Melissa?" Lauren asked. "How does her hair look? Did Stephanie yank it out?"

"No, she did a really good job on it, actually," I said. "The problem is, Melissa thinks she's ready for the Miss Pre-Teen America Contest now. Oops — here she comes. So, anyway, I was wondering if we should — "

Melissa ran up the stairs and down the hall toward me — until she tripped on the phone cord. She caught her fall with her hands and only landed on her knees, skidding to a stop in front of me.

"Lauren — you just missed a great trick," I joked.

There was silence on the other end of the line. I fiddled with the phone, then checked the cord. Sure enough, it had been yanked out of the wall — by Melissa.

"Now look what you've done!" I cried. "Why

don't you slow down and watch where you're going?" I was sick of her dashing up and down the hallway all the time.

"What's wrong?" she asked innocently.

"What's wrong is that you disconnected the phone, and I was talking to Lauren!" I got up and plugged the cord back into the wall. "She's going to think I hung up on her."

"I didn't mean to — it was an accident." Melissa stood up and brushed off the knees of her jeans.

I dialed Lauren's number and frowned at Melissa. "I hope you're not going to stand there and listen to me talk."

Melissa glared at me. "Why are you so mean all the time?" she cried. Then she ran into her room and slammed the door.

"Whoa — what was that?" Lauren asked, coming onto the line.

I sighed. "The usual. Melissa pulled the phone cord out of the wall — sorry. A couple of minutes ago I was starting to think that maybe she wasn't so bad after all! I must have been losing my mind."

Lauren laughed. "Probably!"

"She's driving me crazy!" I said.

"Let's talk about it at the next sleepover," Lauren suggested. "Maybe Patti can give you some tips."

"I know one good thing about the sleepover," I said. "It's at your house this week. It'll be like a vacation . . . far, far away from Melissa. . . .''

"Or at least across town," Lauren added.

"I'd better not tell her where you live," I said. "She might show up and ask Stephanie to do her hair!"

Chapter 6

"You want me to *what?*" I stared at the piece of paper in Melissa's hand.

"Give this to Stephanie," she answered. "It's a surprise. I painted it myself."

It was Friday night and I was on my way out the door. "Okay, I'll give it to her," I told Melissa, folding it quickly and stuffing it into my knapsack.

"Don't tear it!" I heard Melissa cry as I dashed out to Mom's car.

I got to Lauren's house at exactly seven o'clock. "Right on time, as usual!" Mrs. Hunter said when she opened the door. "Are you ever late, Kate?"

"No," I said truthfully. "Unless it's someone else's fault."

She shook her head and laughed. "Go on up — you know where Lauren is."

You have to know where Lauren's room is —

otherwise, you could never find it! Her parents aren't messy at all, but Lauren and Roger leave their stuff all over the place. I stepped on about three sweatshirts on my way up the stairs. I knocked on Lauren's door and walked in.

"What happened?" I asked. "Was there an earthquake on this side of town?"

Lauren looked up from the book she was reading. "What are you talking about?" She was lying on her bed next to her cat, Rocky.

"Your room! It's even worse than usual." I picked up a few notebooks from the floor and put them on her desk.

"Is it?" Lauren replied. "I hadn't noticed."

"I'll help you pick up before Patti and Stephanie get here," I volunteered. "Otherwise there won't be any place to sleep."

"Okay," Lauren said. "But we'd better hurry."

It only took us about ten minutes to put everything away. The room wasn't exactly spotless when we were done, but at least you could see the floor again.

Patti and Stephanie showed up at about seven-fifteen.

"Sorry we're late," Stephanie said, setting down her sleeping bag. "I had to load the dishwasher after dinner."

"No problem," said Lauren.

We all spread our stuff out on the floor. "Now what?" asked Patti.

"There's a terrific double feature on at eight," I told everybody. "It's on 'Friday Night Chillers' on Channel 21. First they're showing *Wait Until Dark*, and after that, *Bunny Lake Is Missing*."

"I've never heard of either one of them," Stephanie said, stretching out on Lauren's bed.

"Neither have I," said Lauren. "Speaking of movies, did you bring the camcorder?"

"Of course!" I gently pulled it out of my knapsack. When I did, the paper Melissa gave me came out, too. "Oh, Stephanie, this is for you," I said.

She leaned down and took it from me. "What is it?"

I shrugged. "I don't know. Melissa asked me to give it to you."

Stephanie studied the picture for a moment. "Oh, this is so cute!" she exclaimed. "She drew a picture of me."

I saw Patti and Lauren exchange glances. They obviously thought it was as weird as I did!

"That's a picture of you?" I said.

"Sure! She's pretty good at painting for a kid her age."

"I wish all she did was paint," I said. "Like last

night, she disconnected the phone. Then this morning, she tried to use the camcorder to film us eating breakfast."

"What's so horrible about that?" Stephanie said.

"She could have broken the camera," I said.

"You're always saying that, but she hasn't done anything to it yet," Stephanie pointed out.

"That's only because she's been incredibly lucky," I reminded her.

"Why don't you give her a break?" Stephanie sat up and swung her legs over the edge of the bed. "She's not that bad."

I rolled my eyes. "I should know what *my* sister's like," I said. "That reminds me — I still want to get your sister and brother in the movie."

"Why do they need to be in the movie?" Stephanie asked. "You're not putting Melissa in the movie."

I frowned. "I didn't say that."

"That's what she thinks," Stephanie said. "She says you don't want her in the movie. And if she's not in it, then I don't see why the twins should be."

"Uh, I don't think Roger wants to be in it!" Lauren said with a little laugh. She and Patti had been sitting there the whole time, listening to us. "He'd probably die of embarrassment if he was on TV with us!"

"So would Horace," Patti added. "He hates

50

having his picture taken! He always runs and hides behind the sofa or a tree or whatever."

I could tell Patti and Lauren were trying to lighten up the conversation, but I was still kind of irritated with Stephanie.

"The twins are too young to mind having their picture taken," I told her. "So what day would be good for me to come over to your house?" I got out a pencil and my pocket datebook.

Stephanie let out a loud sigh. "All right, use them if you want to. But don't expect me to stand there and hold them for you!"

"So, is anyone hungry?" Lauren stood up and rubbed her hands together. "How about some peanut-butter-and-fudge ice cream?"

"Sounds great!" Patti said. "I brought some oatmeal-raisin cookies, too."

"Let's get the food, and then we can play a new game I have — it's called Picture This," said Lauren.

"Don't get me any ice cream," Stephanie said, leaning back on the bed.

"Am I hearing things?" Lauren pretended to faint. "Did you just say you didn't want any of your favorite flavor of ice cream — the kind with the big hunks of chocolate in it, the kind you once said you'd be willing to sit next to Wayne Miller for?"

"Yech!" Patti grimaced. "No ice cream's that good!" She and Lauren started laughing.

But Stephanie just twirled a lock of her hair around her finger. "I'm not hungry," she said.

Lauren looked at Patti and shrugged. "How about you, Kate?"

"Come to think of it, I'm not very hungry, either," I said. It was true. "You could bring me something to drink, though."

"Okay — we'll be right back," Patti promised.

After they left, Stephanie just lay there, playing with her hair. But I couldn't think of anything to say to her, either. Instead, I doodled in my notebook and started making a list of the things I wanted to do over the weekend. I was glad when Stephanie leaned over and turned on Lauren's radio. The silence was getting to me.

Patti and Lauren came back upstairs a few minutes later. "We brought up all the cookies — you might be hungry later," Patti said with a smile. She set down the plate.

"Drinks for everyone!" Lauren announced with a flourish. She broke apart a six-pack of Dr Pepper and gave us each a can. "Ready to draw?"

Patti giggled. "You sound like a cowboy!"

"All right, partners," Lauren said, doing her best imitation of John Wayne. She put her thumbs in her jeans pockets and walked around the room. "It's time for the showdown."

We all started laughing — even Stephanie.

"How does this game work, anyway?" I asked her.

"We split up into teams," Lauren said. She grabbed the game from her desk and sat down on the floor. "Then we draw things, and the other team has to guess what they are."

"Couldn't you just do that with a piece of paper?" Stephanie commented. "I mean, you don't need to buy a game to do that."

"True," said Lauren, "but this game comes with all these cards for ideas of things you could draw, and shows you how to keep score."

"Not everyone's as smart as we are," Patti said, holding her head up in the air. "They need help thinking up things to draw."

"Plus, this comes with a neat drawing board that erases." Lauren demonstrated by writing her name and then pulling the plastic sheet away. "That way, you don't waste paper."

"I guess," said Stephanie, moving down to the floor. "But I still think you could play with a Magic Marker and a drawing pad."

She was really in a bad mood — she was disagreeing with everything.

"What can I say? My grandmother gave it to me," Lauren explained. "I'm not complaining."

"So, who wants to go first?" Patti asked. "Stephanie, why don't you and I be Team One, and Kate and Lauren can be Team Two."

"Are we ready, Team Two?" Lauren said, scooting over to sit next to me.

"Sure — partner," I said.

"Let's not use the cards, okay?" Patti suggested. "Let's just draw the things we want to."

"We have to time how long it takes for the other team to guess what the picture is," Lauren said.

"I'll time you guys," Patti said, "and Stephanie can draw."

Stephanie and Patti held a short conference to decide what to draw. Then Patti nodded, and Stephanie picked up the special pencil. "Ready?" she said.

We nodded.

"Okay, go!" Patti yelled.

Stephanie started by drawing a shirt, then some pants. Then she added something that looked like a pizza. Lauren and I stared at each other. "What?" Lauren said. "What is that?"

"Not the correct answer," Patti said. "Forty-three seconds, forty-four . . ."

Next Stephanie drew some lines that looked like a building, then she drew arrows to connect the clothes and the pizza to the building.

I tried to think the way Stephanie would. What was the first thing that would come to her mind?

Clothes . . . food . . . boys . . . "The mall!" I cried.

"Right!" Patti shrieked. "Seventy-four seconds."

Lauren slapped her forehead. "I should have known — the mall!"

"I can't wait — I'm going there tomorrow," Stephanie admitted with a grin. "It'll be my first Saturday at the mall in three weeks!"

"I know, I can't wait either," said Lauren. "I want to get some long underwear to wear when I go running. What time do you guys want to head over there?"

"Actually, I can't go with you," Stephanie said calmly. "I promised Melissa I'd take her."

I dropped my watch. I'm sure my jaw was hanging open.

"I thought we were all going together," Patti said.

"I know, but when Melissa was over at my house we listened to the new Heat tape, and she really liked it. So I told her we'd pick one up for her this weekend." She glanced at me. "I hope you don't mind."

"Mind? Why should I mind?" I said. "Just because she has the same clothes as you, she wants to wear her hair the same way, now she likes the same stupid group — " Actually, I like Heat, too. But enough is enough!

"I can't help it if Melissa likes the same things I do," Stephanie said. "She just has good taste."

"Yeah, right!" I snorted. "You just tell her what to do!"

"I do not," Stephanie protested. "She makes up her own mind. She's a smart kid."

"Maybe she is," said Lauren slowly, "but why are you spending so much time with her these days? I mean, she has her own friends."

"And so do you," added Patti.

"I know. But right now, I don't know — I can't explain it, but it's like Melissa looks up to me. I can't let her down." Stephanie looked at Patti. "You know how it is with Horace — you want to show him the ropes."

"Speaking of little kids, Stephanie," I said through gritted teeth, "what about Emma and Jeremy?"

Stephanie didn't answer for a second. Then she said, "You know what? I'm sick of this game." She put down the drawing board and the pencil, then climbed up onto Lauren's bed.

"Okay," Lauren said, "how about catching one of those scary movies?" Now I *knew* things were serious. Lauren *hates* scary movies.

"Sure," Patti said, "why not?"

Lauren put the game away and flicked on the TV. Her parents let her move it up to her room whenever we're having a sleepover. "All right!" she said, turning up the volume. The movie was just beginning and the music was incredibly creepy. She jumped up and turned off the overhead light.

"Anyone want a cookie?" Patti held out the plate.

"I'm still not hungry," I said.

Suddenly the light by Lauren's bed went on. I turned around.

"I think I'm going to read," Stephanie said, pulling a paperback out of her overnight bag. "Can you turn down the volume a little?"

"Uh, sure," Lauren said, adjusting the volume.

"What good is a scary movie without scary music?" I muttered.

Lauren and Patti glanced nervously at each other. I knew what they were thinking. This was one of our worst sleepovers ever. I definitely wouldn't be shooting any film tonight. Talk about a horror movie! I'd call it *Stephanie, the Wet Blanket: Part III.*

Chapter
7

"I wish Stephanie were with us," Patti said as we walked into the mall. "I could use her advice on a new pair of jeans. Can you believe it? I grew out of my old ones already."

"I'm kind of glad she didn't come along," I said. "To tell you the truth, she's been getting on my nerves lately."

"I know — the whole Melissa thing," said Lauren. "She was being kind of a drag last night."

"Yeah, that wasn't exactly one of the best sleepovers we've ever had," agreed Patti.

That was for sure. After the movie, we'd played a game of Truth or Dare, which is usually Stephanie's favorite thing to do at a sleepover. But this time she asked really boring questions — things she already knew the answer to! — and she moped around the rest of the night. The only thing that had perked her up was when she put on her new Heat tape. Then she left Lauren's house right after breakfast without another word about her trip to the mall with Melissa. I didn't even know what time they were planning to go. I hoped later in the afternoon — it was around eleven o'clock now.

"I think she got upset when you were talking about the twins," Lauren said to me.

"So it's my fault she's acting like a jerk?" I said.

"I didn't say that!" Lauren stopped at the water fountain and took a drink. "But obviously the twins are bothering her more than usual lately."

"And the way she's hanging all over Melissa is bothering *me*," I said.

"I don't know why she's doing that," said Patti. "Maybe she feels lonely."

I threw up my hands. "How can she feel lonely? She has us!"

"Maybe she really does like Melissa," said Lauren. "That's what she says. Kate, didn't you say that you thought maybe Melissa had grown up a little?"

"Yeah, some of the time," I said, "but the rest of the time she still acts like a five-year-old."

"You mean, an eight-year-old," Patti corrected me.

"No, I don't! Look, let's not talk about this anymore," I said. "It's Saturday, and we're supposed to be having fun." One thing I always do is make sure I have fun on the weekend.

"You should have brought the camera," Patti whispered. She pointed across the walkway at Mark Freedman and Henry Larkin. They are also in our class at school.

"Don't worry — I'm going to bring it to school one day this week," I told her. "We have to put 5B in the movie!"

"Wait — won't that make it a *B*-movie?" Lauren joked.

"Very funny," I said, smiling. That Lauren.

We turned the corner and started heading for Just Juniors, our favorite clothing store. It's in the west wing of the mall. The mall in Riverhurst is pretty big. The first couple of times I went to it, I had to use a map to find my way around. Lauren and I always crack up at the little signs that say "You Are Here." If there's one thing we do know, it's where we are!

The mall was crowded, probably because the weather was so rotten. It was about ten degrees outside. I could just imagine what Stephanie would say: "A perfect day for the mall. We won't have to go outside once." I almost missed having Stephanie with us, though I wouldn't admit it to Lauren and Patti. The mall just wasn't the mall without her.

We spent about half an hour in Just Juniors.

None of us ended up getting anything, but it was fun to look.

"Now what?" asked Patti.

"Want to go to Good Sports with me?" Lauren replied.

"Not really," I said, wrinkling my nose. "I might go look in the photography store. I want to ask their advice about how to edit my movie."

Patti tapped her chin. "Why don't we compromise and eat lunch instead?"

Lauren put her arm around Patti's shoulder. "Great idea!"

One of our favorite places is the Pizza Palace. We turned and started walking toward it.

As we passed Totally Audio, I saw a pair of familiar red, black, and white jackets at the register. I felt like not saying hello. If they wanted to spend the day together, then let them!

But Patti spotted them, too. "Look, there're Stephanie and Melissa!" she said. We stopped walking and waited for them to come out of the store. It was bizarre seeing Stephanie and my sister together. I felt a pang in my stomach as I watched them smiling at each other. I tried to tell myself I was just hungry, but I knew that wasn't it. I felt hurt and angry. You just didn't hang out with someone else's little sister. That was one of those unwritten rules everyone knew — everyone except Stephanie.

"Hi, you guys!" Patti said cheerfully.

"Hi!" Stephanie smiled. She seemed as though she were in a much better mood. "Look — the new Silent Whispers tape is out." She took it out of her bag and showed it to us. "It has that new song we like so much."

"Great — we can listen to it at the sleepover at your house next week," Lauren said.

"Look what I got!" Melissa cried. She waved the new Heat tape in front of my face. "Stephanie bought it for me!" she announced proudly.

"She didn't have enough money," Stephanie explained with a shrug.

"We were just going to the Pizza Palace to grab some lunch," Patti said. "Why don't you guys come along?"

I knew Patti was trying to patch things up between us, but I wasn't crazy about the idea of lunch with Stephanie *and* Melissa.

"Yeah, come on," Lauren said. "We can get a large pie."

Stephanie turned to Melissa. "Well?"

"Sure, I love pizza," Melissa answered.

"Then we're off," said Lauren. "Follow me, troops!" Patti and Lauren took the lead and Stephanie and Melissa walked behind them. That left me in back, by myself. I decided not to make a big deal about it, though. I'd just sit there and pretend I didn't mind the latest addition to the Sleepover Friends.

We managed to get five seats together at the Pizza Palace (not that it's a palace — it's more like a fast-food joint). I sat at the opposite end of the counter from Melissa. I could just see her yelling in my ear or throwing a meatball at me. If Stephanie wanted to be humiliated in public, fine — but *I* wasn't going to be.

That was another thing I didn't understand. Since Stephanie was usually so concerned about her image, why would she want to be seen in public with a third-grader? She sure wasn't acting like herself!

John, the cook, brought our pizza over to the counter. "And who's this?" he asked, putting down some paper plates in front of Melissa.

"Melissa Beekman," she said shyly.

"Nice to meet you, Melissa Beekman. Are you Kate's sister?" John asked.

Melissa nodded.

"Welcome to the Pizza Palace," John said. "Enjoy your meal."

"Thank you," she said. Then she passed the paper plates around to all of us. Talk about not acting like herself! I had never seen Melissa be so polite and, well, non-obnoxious in her life.

I grabbed a piece of the double-cheese-and-meatball pie and took a big bite. At least John's pizza was still the same — terrific!

I watched Melissa as she ate her pizza. Usually she pulls all the cheese off the top to see how long it will stretch out. I couldn't wait to see Stephanie's reaction to that.

But Melissa just sat there and ate her pizza like the rest of us. She even wiped her mouth with her napkin a few times.

"So what are you guys doing the rest of the afternoon?" Patti asked Stephanie.

"I have to go to the supermarket with my mom." Stephanie rolled her eyes.

"Can I come?" Melissa asked.

Stephanie shook her head. "It won't be any fun. Last week when we went, Jeremy started howling in the middle of the supermarket and he wouldn't stop."

"I know — my friend Eileen has a baby brother and he's so-o-o-o loud," Melissa said.

"Look who's talking," I muttered. Actually, Melissa wasn't being loud, for once. She was behaving herself. I wished I had the video camera along — so I could record this important moment in history!

A few minutes later, Taylor Sprouse and his friends strolled into the restaurant. Taylor was wearing a new addition to his all-black wardrobe — a black leather jacket.

I was sure that Stephanie was going to die of embarrassment. I knew she wanted Taylor to think she was cool. And being seen with Melissa was definitely *not* cool.

Watching Melissa was kind of like watching a time bomb. I knew she was going to do something disastrous, but I didn't know what, or when.

Taylor and his friends completely ignored us, as usual. They think being in sixth grade makes them incredibly special.

When Taylor walked past us, Melissa leaned forward and whispered, "Is he going to a funeral?"

I burst out laughing, and so did Lauren and Patti. Even Stephanie cracked up, and she hates it when we make fun of Taylor.

Taylor sneered in our direction. "What's so funny, dweebheads?" he said.

"Uh, nothing," Stephanie said. "Nothing at all."

Then she turned back around to the counter and we all started laughing again. Melissa stuck out her tongue at Taylor's back and for some reason, that made me laugh even harder. It was the perfect response for a jerk like him.

Maybe Melissa was going to be a comedian when she grew up.

That night I had nothing to do, so I called Lauren. We started talking about Stephanie and how happy she had seemed when she was at the mall with Melissa. She'd been positively bored at our sleepover the night before!

"Do you think she likes Melissa more than us?" I asked.

"I don't think so," said Lauren. "But you have to admit, Melissa wasn't bad today. I mean, I've never seen her like that."

"You mean nice, funny, and well-behaved?" I said.

"Exactly." Lauren laughed. "I love that joke she made about Taylor. She was really funny!"

"Yeah," I said. "And you know what else? I've been thinking. Maybe she *has* changed, grown up or whatever."

"It happens to everybody," Lauren said. "Sooner or later."

"Yeah, but overnight?" I asked. "It was only a couple of days ago that she pelted me with that snowball." Just the thought of that ice trickling down my back made me shiver.

"*We* still have snowball fights," Lauren pointed out. "That doesn't mean she's not grown up."

I twisted the phone cord with my fingers. "I guess so."

After I talked to Lauren, I called Patti to see what she thought. Since she has a younger brother, I considered her an expert on the situation.

"So is Melissa a new person or what?" I asked after we talked about what had happened at the mall.

"All I know is, that's the first time I've seen her act so grown up," Patti commented. "Maybe her monster days *are* over."

When we finished talking, I went to my room and looked at myself in the mirror. If Melissa was growing up, that meant I was getting older, too. But I still looked the same. Short.

Then I heard a blast of music coming from Melissa's room. After a few notes I recognized the song — it was from the new Heat album.

I made my decision. If Melissa was growing up and needing someone to show her the ropes, then that person was going to be *me* — not Stephanie. I was the one she should be taking after.

Tomorrow, I thought, tomorrow we'll start doing stuff together. I got out a notebook and started making a list of things we could do.

Even if it killed me, I was going to be nice to Melissa. I wanted my sister back!

Chapter 8

I woke up early on Sunday. I couldn't wait to start "Be Nice to Melissa Day." It was only going to be a matter of time before Melissa stopped imitating Stephanie and started imitating me!

Even the weather was on my side. For the first time in days, it was nice outside — the sun was shining, and the temperature was above freezing.

When Melissa and my parents came downstairs for breakfast, I had already set the table and poured the orange juice. "Good morning!" I said, pulling out Melissa's chair for her.

"Hi," she mumbled sleepily.

"Good morning, Kate," my father said, smiling. "Up with the birds today, are we?"

"What's with the tie, Dad?" I asked. My mom was dressed up, too, in a dress and high heels. "Are you guys going somewhere today?"

My mother nodded as she plugged in the coffee maker. "We're going to visit some friends from college who live in Morrisville. It's about a one-and-a-half hour's drive."

"I don't want to go," Melissa said with a frown. "I hate long car rides."

I didn't want to go, either — I had big plans for the day.

"That's okay — we decided we would leave you two here," my dad said. "Do you think you can handle that, Kate?"

I nodded eagerly. "Sure — it'll be fun."

My mother and father gave me a strange look.

"It's such a nice day, we'll find lots to do," I told them. "When will you be back?"

"Around five o'clock," my mom said.

"No problem!" I said, putting the cereal boxes on the table. "Everything's under control."

I knocked on Melissa's door, even though I knew she wouldn't hear me. She was playing her new cassette so loudly, I couldn't even hear myself knock!

I walked into her room. She was jumping up and down on top of her bed in time to the music. I walked over to her tape player and turned down the volume.

"Hey!" she cried.

"Hey, yourself," I said. "Listen, I was wondering if you wanted to go see a movie this afternoon."

Melissa shook her head.

"Are you sure? The new Disney movie is playing at the mall," I told her.

She shook her head again. Okay, so maybe I wasn't going to turn my sister into a movie fanatic like me. That was probably a good thing — one director in the family was enough.

"All right, then . . . how about going sledding in the park?" I offered. "We can bring the toboggan and go down the big hill together."

"No," Melissa said in a bored voice. She hopped off her bed and walked over to the tape player and turned the volume up a few notches.

Usually Melissa jumps at the chance to do things with me — and she usually didn't wait for an invitation, either. What was with her? I took my list out of my pocket and skimmed it. "Okay, how about if we go to the roller-skating rink? It's really fun — they play music and lots of kids go," I said.

"I wouldn't like it," Melissa said.

"How do you know if you haven't tried it?" I asked.

"Trust me," she said. Great — now she was talking like Stephanie, too.

"Well, what *do* you want to do?" I said, stuffing my list back into my pocket. "I'm open to anything."

"I want to go to Stephanie's house," she answered.

70

Anything except that, I thought to myself. "You can't," I said briskly. Here I was, trying as hard as I could to be nice to her, and all she wanted was to spend time with Stephanie! "Why not?" she pouted.

"Mom and Dad want us to stay around the house," I said.

"Then how come you said we could go to all those other places?" Melissa asked.

"Never mind," I said through clenched teeth.

"Well, if I have to stay here, then I want Eileen to come over," Melissa said. She walked out into the hallway and picked up the phone.

She was acting like staying in the house with me all day would be pure torture. I went into my room and shut the door. I felt like I was going to start crying. A few weeks ago, Melissa would have done anything to hang out with me. Now I was the plague!

It really hurt that she wanted to be with everyone except me. The more I thought about it, the more I realized that she was treating me the same way I had always treated her. Whenever she had wanted to do stuff with me, I had told her no.

Now she had found someone who wanted to do things with her — Stephanie. And she didn't need me — or want me — around anymore. I had told her to get lost too many times. It was my own fault that she was turning into a miniature Stephanie.

I wasn't going to give up, though. I still had a

few tricks up my sleeve. I was going to win Melissa back if I had to eat peanut-butter-and-jelly every meal of the day and sit through twelve straight hours of *Sesame Street*!

"If I hear that song one more time," I muttered, tapping my fingers against the windowpane. Melissa and Eileen were in her room, and they were listening to that stupid Heat tape for the ninth time in a row. (Yes, I counted.) I thought I was going to go crazy. A while ago I had suggested that we all get out of the house and go skating, but they weren't interested. They said they had more important things to do. Like what? I wondered. They hadn't left the room for over an hour.

Then I remembered what Mom does when she wants to find out what me and my friends were up to. She barges in — but she does it nicely.

I went down to the kitchen and put some chocolate-chip cookies — Melissa's favorite — on a plate. Then I poured two big glasses of milk, put everything on a tray, and headed back upstairs.

I pounded on the door with my free hand. "Melissa! It's me, can I come in?"

All I could hear on the other side of the door — besides "You've Broken My Heartstrings" for at least the fifteenth time — was lots of giggles.

I turned the knob and walked into her bedroom.

Eileen was sitting on a chair in front of the mirror, and Melissa was standing behind her — putting Mom's big curlers in her hair! And Melissa's hair was already all wrapped up in curlers. Not very neatly, but it was going to be very curly! Now the beauty shop was at my house. Why hadn't Melissa asked me to curl her hair if that was what she wanted?

When the song ended, I cleared my throat loudly and they turned around. Their eyes lit up when they saw the cookies, and Eileen jumped out of her chair. She looked pretty funny — half of her hair was stuck in the curlers, and the other half was dripping wet. At the rate she was going, Melissa was definitely not going to be a hairdresser!

Eileen grabbed three cookies. "Yum!" she said.

"Melissa, how about you?" I said as kindly as I could.

She wrinkled her nose. "Do we have anything else?"

"These are chocolate-chip," I told her. "Your favorite!"

"Not anymore," she said. She took one of the glasses of milk and sipped it.

I took a deep breath. It's hard for me to keep my cool sometimes. "What is, then?" I asked her.

"Peanut-butter-chocolate-chip," she said. "You know, the kind Stephanie makes."

"*She* doesn't make them," I said slowly. I could

73

feel my face getting hot. "Her mom does."

"Whatever," Melissa said with a wave of her hand. "You should taste them, Eileen — they're so-o-o-o good."

Eileen looked up at me and ran a handful of crumbs through her wet hair. "Do you know how to make them?"

"No, I don't," I admitted. "I make great superfudge, though. Do you guys want some of that?" I could make good things to eat, too!

Melissa shook her head. "I've had that about a million times."

"Fine," I said tightly. "That's just fine. I'll leave this stuff here in case you get hungry." I walked over to Melissa's dresser and set it down. Then suddenly I had a brainstorm. I knew a surefire way to get Melissa to do something with me — and Eileen, too. "Hey, I have a great idea!" I said, turning around.

Melissa looked at me skeptically, arms folded across her chest. "What?" she asked.

"Well, you know how I'm making that home movie for the TV competition, right? Why don't I film you guys — you know, before and after your makeovers?" I smiled. There was no way Melissa could turn down this opportunity — she was a real ham.

Melissa seemed to be thinking it over. Then she whispered something in Eileen's ear. Eileen nodded.

"Okay, I'll go get the video camera!" I said cheerfully.

Melissa shook her head. "We don't want to be in the movie."

"But you've been bugging me all week to put you in it!" I reminded her.

"We have something else we have to do," Melissa interrupted.

"Oh, and what's that?" I asked, tapping my foot against the carpet. "Are you going to listen to that Heat tape another nine times?"

"*No,*" Melissa replied in a bratty tone, "we're not. And we're not going to tell you what we're doing, either."

"Fine!" I said. "If you think there's something more important than being on TV, then go ahead!" I had told myself I wasn't going to get angry with her, but who could blame me? She was impossible! I marched across the room toward the door.

The next thing I knew, my foot slipped on something and I crashed to the floor. "Ow!" I yelled, rubbing my hip.

Melissa and Eileen were laughing hysterically.

I looked around to see what I had stepped on. "You shouldn't leave these lying around," I said through gritted teeth. "Someone could get hurt."

That only made them laugh harder.

That did it! "Be Nice to Melissa Day" was now officially over!

I spent the afternoon reading a book I'd gotten out of the library that described how to make "The Best" home movie. Suddenly I heard a loud shriek coming from the bathroom. I decided to ignore it. Then I heard a burst of giggles. Next I heard footsteps thunder down the hallway and stop outside my door. Then Eileen said, "Should we show her?"

The next thing I knew, she and Melissa jumped into my room, yelling "Ta-da!"

They were holding up red T-shirts — only the shirts were wet, and they were dripping all over the floor! "What did you guys do?" I asked them.

"We made these shirts," Melissa announced. "Just like Stephanie's!"

Here we go again, I thought to myself. "You mean, you dyed them?" I asked.

Melissa nodded.

"With what?" I asked.

"Red stuff, silly!" Melissa rolled her eyes. "We put them in the bathtub and then we put the red stuff in. Don't they look great?"

I looked at the T-shirts. They did look nice, but they were dripping pink drops all over the place. I jumped up off my bed. "Melissa, the dye is dripping onto the floor!" I grabbed the T-shirts out of their

76

hands. "We have to hang them up in the bathroom until they're dry."

Melissa shrugged. "Okay, I guess."

I ran down the hall to the bathroom, cupping one hand underneath the shirts to catch the drops.

I stopped dead in my tracks when I saw the bathroom. The bathtub was full of red water. The shower curtain was red all around the bottom. There was a trail of red water all around the sink and on the floor. And, worst of all, all of our white towels were now red, pink, or covered with pink spots!

I glanced at my watch. It was four o'clock, and my parents would be home in an hour. If they saw this mess, I'd get in trouble for not watching Melissa closely enough. But I couldn't clean it all by myself!

"Melissa!" I yelled. "Come here!"

She didn't answer. I ran through the house looking for her, and got downstairs just in time to see her and Eileen run out the door, carrying their sleds. "That figures," I muttered to myself.

I picked up the phone and called Lauren. "There's an emergency!" I told her when she answered the phone. "Can you come over to my house right away?"

"Sure," Lauren said. "What's the emergency?"

"I'll tell you when you get here," I said. "We don't have much time."

"Okay," Lauren agreed. "I'll be right over."

Chapter
9

"What happened when your parents got home?" Lauren asked me Monday at school.

"I was so lucky! I was taking the towels out of the dryer *just* as they walked in the door. There were still some spots on them, so I dumped them into the washing machine, you know, to run them through a second time. And my mother said, 'Oh, Kate, how nice of you to do the laundry while we were gone.' " I laughed.

"What are you guys talking about?" Stephanie wanted to know.

"My parents went away yesterday and left me in charge. Melissa and Eileen decided to do a little fashion designing. They tried to dye some white T-shirts red," I explained. "Actually, the shirts came out fine — but the bathroom was a mess. Lauren and

78

Patti came over and helped me clean up. I called you, but you weren't home," I said.

Stephanie sighed. "Yeah, I know. We took a trip into the city to see my grandparents," Stephanie said.

"So what's so terrible about that?" Patti asked. "You usually love seeing them."

"Yeah, don't they always give you some really cool present?" Lauren commented. "And take you out to lunch at great restaurants?"

Stephanie nodded. "That's just it. Number one, we did go out to eat. And everyone in the restaurant fussed over Emma and Jeremy. *Then*, we went back to their house and opened about two thousand presents — for the twins."

"So things at home haven't gotten any better?" Patti asked with a concerned look.

"Nope," said Stephanie. "It gets worse all the time. Tomorrow I have to baby-sit while my mom goes to get her hair cut."

"Just keep thinking about the sleepover this week," Lauren told her. "We'll be out at your apartment and you won't be able to hear Emma or Jeremy all night!"

"Don't be so sure," Stephanie replied. "Have you ever heard them cry?"

* * *

The next few days kind of flew by. I was working hard to finish the movie — it was due to WRIV in a week, and I still had a lot to do on it. I brought the camera to school on Thursday and filmed some of the kids in our class. The cafeteria shots were the best. Everyone looks pretty funny when they're eating.

After school, we all went back to my house to work on the film. Stephanie and Melissa hadn't been hanging out so much this week, because Stephanie was so busy at home. Melissa had spent another afternoon at Stephanie's house, though, and she was still wearing red, black, and white all the time. And if she listened to that Heat tape one more time, it would break. Or I would break her tape player!

I'd decided that "A Day in the Life of a Fifth-Grader" needed a scene where we sat around and talked about what it meant to be in the fifth grade — you know, like they do in those serious, documentary films.

"What are we supposed to *say?*" Lauren asked. "This is ridiculous."

"Just relax. Talk about how the fifth grade is different from the fourth grade. And move over a little on the couch," I told her, "so I can get all of you in the same shot."

Lauren sighed and scooted over next to Patti.

"Ready? Lights, camera . . . action!" I cried.

Nobody said anything. Patti was staring at the

floor, while Lauren flipped through a magazine. Stephanie just looked right at the camera and smiled.

I waved my arm at them and mouthed, "Come on!"

"Being a fifth-grader . . . it's intense," Lauren said with a serious look.

"Yes," agreed Stephanie. "It is quite an experience. Don't you agree, Professor Jenkins?"

Patti cracked up laughing.

"Cut!" I yelled. "All right, so we won't do the interview thing."

"Good!" Lauren leaned back and sighed.

The front door slammed, and Melissa ran into the living room. "Hi!" she said. "Stephanie, look at the shirt I made." She pointed at her red T-shirt.

Stephanie glanced at me. "Yeah, I heard about this." She smiled at Melissa. "You did a nice job. It looks great."

"It's just like yours," Melissa told her.

Stephanie nodded.

"Well, what do you guys want to put in the movie, if we're not going to do the interviews?" I asked. I didn't feel like standing around and listening to the Mutual Admiration Society.

"We could bake something," Lauren suggested. "Or make some of your super-fudge, Kate."

"And then we could film you eating it afterward!" I laughed.

"We could play a game of Truth or Dare and film it," said Lauren.

"No way!" Patti cried. "Do you want everyone in Riverhurst to know your deepest, darkest secrets?"

Melissa and I have been working on something for the movie," Stephanie announced.

"Really? What?" asked Patti.

"A dance!" Melissa said excitedly.

"We've been rehearsing a dance and lip-synch routine," Stephanie explained. "Can we do it in the movie?"

"Wait — let me guess," I said. "It's to one of Heat's songs, right?"

"Yeah," Stephanie said. "How did you know?"

I shook my head. "Never mind. Okay, you can do it," I told them. If I didn't let them, Melissa would hate me forever. I had to at least be reasonable. "Go get the tape."

Melissa bolted up the stairs and returned with the tape. We cleared a space in the living room for them, put the tape in the tape player, and stood back to watch.

They started out with a little hop to the left and then to the right, and then they started mouthing to the music. I hated to admit it, but they looked pretty good. So that's what Melissa had been doing, listening to that tape nonstop! Why hadn't she told me she was working on a dance routine? Okay, so maybe dancing wasn't a specialty of mine, but I could have given her *some* pointers.

Maybe not, I thought, as I filmed them. Stephanie was a much better dancer than I was. And watching Melissa, I realized she was, too! So my little sister was a comedienne, a dancer . . . what next?

"Wait!" Stephanie suddenly yelled. "You're supposed to go this way," she told Melissa, taking her arm.

Melissa stopped dancing and looked up at Stephanie. "This is boring," she said. "We do it the same way every time. I want to do a different dance," Melissa said stubbornly.

"Okay," said Stephanie, "but not now. Kate's filming us!"

"Actually, I stopped the tape when you stopped dancing," I said. But Melissa had already turned and run upstairs.

"What's with her?" Stephanie asked.

"Don't ask *me*," I said. "You're her dance partner."

Melissa came back downstairs with her teddy bear. "Noggin has to be in the movie!" she announced.

"Okay," I agreed.

"But first, let's finish our dance," Stephanie said. She took Noggin from Melissa and put him on the couch. Then she rewound the Heat tape, and started playing it again. "You can turn the camera back on now," she told me.

When the song began, Stephanie did all the same moves she had done the first time. But Melissa did a little dance over to the couch, picked up Noggin, and twirled him around. Instead of singing to the camera, she sang the song to Noggin as she danced around the living room with him.

"No!" Stephanie cried. "This is all wrong." She put her hands on her hips. "Kate, can you cut all that from the movie?"

"Sure," I said. I could, but I wasn't going to! They looked pretty funny, doing their separate dances. Patti and Lauren were standing behind me, and I could hear them giggling. I was relieved to see that Melissa didn't go along with Stephanie's ideas *all* the time.

Stephanie walked over to Melissa, who was still bopping around the room. "Do it the way we rehearsed it, okay?" she said. "Only babies play with bears."

Melissa stopped dancing. "That's not true," she said. She looked like she was going to start crying.

Patti stepped out from behind the camera. "You're right, Melissa. You know what? I have a bear, too. I played with him all the time last year, and I still keep him in my room. I have a huge collection of stuffed animals!'' She smiled at Melissa.

Good old Patti, I thought, *she always saves the day.* "Yeah, there's hardly any room for Patti in there!'' I joked.

We all laughed — everyone except Stephanie.

She was busy rewinding the tape again. "Look, can we get back to the dance routine?'' she said in an irritated voice.

"Sure,'' I said, a little surprised. "I'm ready.''

Stephanie got into position. "Ready, Melissa?''

Melissa walked over to her spot, but she didn't seem too excited about it.

The song started for the third time — by now I knew all the words by heart — and Stephanie did the hop to the left, and then to the right. Melissa hopped to the left — and then picked up Noggin from the floor and wandered off into the kitchen.

Stephanie threw up her hands. "What's her problem?''

"Maybe she's tired,'' I suggested. "She gets cranky when she's tired.'' Or, maybe, I thought, she was getting sick of doing everything the way Stephanie wanted it done.

"She ruined the whole movie,'' Stephanie said, stopping the cassette with a click.

Before I could defend my sister — it wasn't her fault Stephanie was trying to make her into the next dance sensation of the world — the phone rang. It was Mrs. Green, and she sounded as if she was in as bad a mood as Stephanie!

"I'm looking for Stephanie," she said. "She was supposed to be home an hour ago. Is she there, by any chance?"

"Uh, sure," I said

"Just tell her that I want her to come home immediately, if not sooner. Thanks, Kate," Mrs. Green said.

"You're welcome," I said. I hung up the phone. "That was your mom," I told Stephanie. "She wants you to go home immediately, and I quote."

"Oh, great!" Stephanie grumbled. She started putting on her jacket. "What a terrific afternoon."

"Hang in there," Lauren said. "Tomorrow's the sleepover escape, remember?"

"Yeah," Stephanie said. "At least then I'll be off duty!" She picked up her knapsack and walked to the door. "See you guys tomorrow," she said.

"So much for finishing the movie," I said once she was gone.

"Is that all you care about, your movie?" asked Lauren. "Stephanie's really upset!"

"I know," I said. "But what can *we* do about it?"

"I don't know," said Patti, "but I'm going to think of something!"

Chapter
10

"You're *not* going to believe this!" Stephanie tossed her knapsack onto her chair at school the next morning. "It's the most unbelievable thing that's ever happened."

"What?" asked Patti.

"The sleepover tonight? It's cancelled," Stephanie said with an angry huff. "Called off! Not going to happen! History!"

"How come?" Lauren asked.

"My parents think I should be punished for being late yesterday," Stephanie complained. "Isn't that the most ridiculous thing you've ever heard?"

"It does seem like you pitch in a lot at home," I commented.

"I know!" She shook her head. "I feel like Cinderella!"

"Are you grounded, or it is just for tonight?" asked Patti.

"Who knows," Stephanie muttered. "I'll probably never be able to go to another sleepover!"

Mrs. Mead walked into the classroom then. "We'll figure out a way to get you out of this," Lauren whispered before we went back to our seats.

"I don't think you can!" Stephanie said.

"We have to," Patti said. "Sleepover Friends forever, remember?"

"Nothing lasts forever," Stephanie said, frowning.

"What are we going to do?" Patti asked. "We have to cheer up Stephanie — she's miserable!"

We were riding our bikes home together after school. Stephanie's mom had picked her up.

"And we have to do something fast," I said. "We can't stop having sleepovers. It's a tradition — we've hardly ever missed a Friday night!"

"I have an idea," said Lauren, kicking at a pile of snow. "Let's have our sleepover tonight — just the three of us."

"And leave Stephanie out?" Patti shook her head. "She wouldn't like that." The last time one of the Sleepover Friends missed a sleepover, it was me — and that started a whole mess of problems.

"The reason we need to have the sleepover is

so we can figure out a way to cheer her up," said Lauren. "So even though she won't be there, we'll be thinking of her the whole time."

"Good idea," I said. Even though I hadn't exactly been thrilled with Stephanie lately, I didn't like seeing her so upset, either. The whole time I'd known her, she'd never been so down in the dumps. I didn't know how we were going to pull her out of it, but we had to try.

"Well . . . okay, I guess," Patti finally said. "But I feel funny having a sleepover without her. She's going to think we don't care that she's grounded."

"No she won't," Lauren insisted. "Because she's not going to know that we're having one."

We all looked at Lauren in surprise.

"It's for a good cause," she argued. "We're not doing it to be mean — we're doing it to help Stephanie."

"There's only one problem," Patti said. "Where are we going to have the sleepover? My parents are having some people over for dinner, so it can't be at my house."

"Mine either," said Lauren. "Roger's having a party with some of his friends."

They turned and looked at me. "I know you've been upset about the way Stephanie sort of took over Melissa," said Patti, "but do you think we could meet at your house?"

I didn't need any time to think it over. When one of us is in trouble, we all pitch in to help. Even though Stephanie had been a better friend to my little sister lately than she had been to me, I still cared about her — a lot. "I'll convince my parents somehow," I said.

"Great!" said Lauren. "Operation Cheer-Up is about to begin!"

"I hope you have some ideas, because I sure don't," I told Lauren when she showed up at my house.

"Don't tell me — you haven't been making a list all afternoon?" Lauren teased.

"I tried to," I admitted, "but I couldn't think of anything."

Patti came over a few minutes later, and we went up to my room.

"Let's get to work," Lauren said. She sat on the floor and opened up her overnight bag. Then she pulled out a paper plate with brownies on it, covered with plastic wrap.

"You call that work?" I said. "I thought we were supposed to be cheering up Stephanie, not pigging out!"

Lauren rolled her eyes. "This is part of the plan, stupid. We're going to bring her a Sleepover Kit tonight! That way, it'll be like she's at the sleepover with us, even though she's at her house and we're here."

"What a terrific idea!" Patti sat down next to her. "What else is there besides brownies?"

"Well . . . I haven't figured that out yet, exactly," Lauren admitted.

"That's okay — we'll think up things together," I said. I was impressed — Lauren's idea for Operation Cheer-Up was really great. I sat down on my bed. "What else do we do at sleepovers?"

"Laugh a lot?" Patti suggested.

"Too bad we don't have one of those cans that makes laughing noises — you know, canned laughter?" Lauren said.

I snapped my fingers. "We'll tape ourselves talking and making jokes and stuff," I said. "When she listens to it, it'll be as if we're in the same room with her."

Patti nodded eagerly. "Good idea!"

I got out my cassette player and found a blank tape. "What are we going to say?" asked Patti.

"Just be yourself," I said, pressing the record button.

"Hi, Stephanie!" we all yelled at the same time. Then we started laughing.

"I'm sure we sound like complete idiots," said Lauren.

"But when don't we?" I asked.

"We wanted to make you this tape so you could see how much fun we're *not* having without you," said Patti.

"At the moment we're just trying to keep Lauren from eating the brownies that are supposed to be for you!" I said.

"Hey, that's not fair," said Lauren. "I haven't touched them!"

"It's only a matter of time before the Bottomless Pit strikes," I said in an eerie voice.

"Want a good laugh, Stephanie?" Lauren asked. "You should see what Kate's room looks like! There's actually a piece of paper on the floor that's supposed to be on her desk. *And*, one of her sweaters is out of place! It's shocking!"

"Call the Neat Police!" Patti said.

We talked into the tape for about ten minutes, and even played a short game of Truth or Dare. Then we ended by singing a song we'd all had to learn for a school recital. We improvised and made up our own words, so it was a lot better than the original version. We made the chorus go, "Oh, Stephanie, where are you?"

"That was great!" I said, shutting off the tape recorder.

"She should get a good laugh out of that," Lauren agreed. "I just hope that tape doesn't fall into the wrong hands someday — it would be humiliating!"

"Okay, now what?" asked Patti.

I looked around my room. "Why don't we each make cards for her?" I said.

"Instead of a get-well card, I'm going to make a get-happy card," Patti said, pulling the cap off a red marker.

"I'm going to make a sympathy card," said Lauren. "Sorry for the loss of your Friday night!"

"What are you going to do?" Patti asked me.

"I don't know." I stared at the blank sheet of paper in front of me. I don't usually go for that flowery stuff. But I wanted to do something different. "It's going to be a funny poem," I said. At least I hoped so! I tapped my pen against the desk. Then I wrote,

The Sleepover Without Stephanie

It was a dark and stormy night
And nothing was going quite right
Stephanie wasn't there
I missed her curly hair
And listening to Lauren sing was a real fright.

We were so bored, we tried to watch TV
But there wasn't anything on, not even a movie
We weren't hungry, so we didn't make the dip
And we didn't even eat one single chip

"Aren't you done yet?" Lauren asked me. "We have to bring the kit over to Stephanie's before it gets too late."

"Not yet," I said. "I have to write a little more." Writing poems was a lot harder than I'd thought!

> The night was a total waste
> Playing Truth or Dare wasn't the same
> Without Stephanie around
> The whole sleepover was pretty lame!

I wrote, We miss you! at the bottom of the card and then signed my name. And I drew three frowning faces at the top of the poem, next to the title. It looked pretty good, if I do say so myself.

"Are you finished?" Lauren asked.

I nodded.

"It's eight-thirty," Patti said. "We'd better get going, anyway. Oh — I almost forgot. I found something this afternoon that I thought might help." She pulled a folded piece of paper out of her bag. "It's an article about how hard it is for kids to adjust when there are new babies in a family."

"Stephanie doesn't have to read that!" I said. "She knows how hard it is."

"I know that," said Patti, "but her parents don't."

"What are you going to do, leave it in their mailbox?" Lauren asked.

"No. I think we should give it to Stephanie to read, so she'll know she's not the only one. Then she can show it to her parents or leave it on the kitchen table or something."

I nodded. "Good idea."

Patti wrote a quick note and attached it to the article. We put everything into a brown paper bag and wrote *Official Sleepover Kit* on the side in big red and black letters. Then we ran downstairs and put on our coats and boots.

"Wait a second! We almost forgot the most important thing!" Lauren cried. She ran into the kitchen and came back carrying a can of Dr Pepper — Stephanie's all-time favorite soda. I slipped it into the bag. "Let's go!"

Chapter 11

"I keep missing!" Lauren complained. She picked up another pebble and threw it at Stephanie's window. It bounced off the wall of the house and fell to the ground.

Patti shivered. "Maybe we should just call her," she said.

"No, I'll get it." Lauren picked up a bigger pebble and tossed it up into the air. It hit Stephanie's bedroom window with a loud "smack!"

"You don't have to break it," I said, grimacing.

As we were staring up at her window, Stephanie pulled the curtains to one side and looked down. When she saw us, she waved and pointed to the back door. We hurried over to it.

"I hope she doesn't get in trouble for this," said Patti.

"Her parents won't mind if we only stay a minute," I said. "We'll be quiet."

A minute later, the back door opened and Stephanie came out wearing her jacket. Even though she had a scarf wrapped around her face, I could tell that she had been crying. Her eyes were pink and her face was a little puffy.

"What are you guys doing here?" she asked in a little voice.

"Since you couldn't come to the sleepover, we decided to bring the sleepover to you!" I announced.

"Here, we made this for you," Lauren said. She held out the Sleepover Kit.

"What is it?" asked Stephanie suspiciously.

"It's the Official Sleepover Kit," I told her. "It has everything you need to have your own sleepover — with us — when we're not there."

"We could never have a sleepover without you," said Patti. "So we came to share it with you."

"There are some excellent brownies in there, and a tape of us to listen to, and — "

"Don't ruin the surprise!" I said.

Stephanie opened the bag and peered inside. "This is so nice of you guys," she said. "I can't believe you came over here. Or that you did all this for me." Her voice was shaking and I was afraid she was going to start crying.

"So, uh, how's it going?" I asked her.

"I've just been in my room, bored to death," she said. "Then I tried to call all of you and either you weren't home, or the line was busy. I felt like the whole world had deserted me!"

"We wouldn't do that," Patti said.

"I know," said Stephanie.

"Well, we'd better go. We don't want to get you in trouble," said Lauren. "Besides, it's freezing out here!"

"I wish you guys could stay." Stephanie glanced back at the house. "But my parents wouldn't go for it. They say I have to prove that I can be responsible first."

"In that case, you'd better prove it soon!" Lauren said. "I mean, we don't want to have to make a Sleepover Kit every week."

"But we will if we have to," Patti said quickly.

"They'll let you have a sleepover next week," I predicted.

Stephanie looked at me. "You really think so?"

"Sure," I said. "Go back to your room and open the bag — you won't be bored after that!"

"Embarrassed to be friends with us, maybe, but not bored!" Patti said with a laugh.

"Okay." Stephanie took a few steps toward the house and then stopped. "Will you guys call me tomorrow?"

"Definitely!" Lauren said, smiling.

"Good night, Stephanie!" I said.

She trudged up the stairs to the door. Then she turned around and said, "Thanks!"

"Any time!" Patti whispered loudly as Stephanie opened the back door and slipped back inside.

"I've never seen her so sad before," I said as we started walking back to my house. "I'm glad we came over."

"I think we did the right thing," Patti agreed.

"In other words, Operation Cheer-Up was a success!" Lauren cried.

Patti and I looked at each other and laughed. "What's next, Lauren?" I said. "Operation Chow-Down?"

"No, Operation Get-Kate!" she said, throwing a handful of snow at me. Then we raced each other all the way back to my house.

Chapter
12

Lauren and Patti left right after breakfast. We all usually have to clean our rooms — well, besides me — on Saturdays, and since I wanted to finish the film that afternoon, they had agreed to go home and clean in the morning.

I was cleaning up the kitchen when Melissa came downstairs. She had been amazingly quiet during our sleepover. She hadn't bothered us once — I guess since Stephanie wasn't there, she wasn't interested.

"What's for breakfast?" she asked, sitting down at the table.

Normally I would have told her to fix it for herself, but I was *still* trying to be nice to her. "How about waffles?" I offered.

She nodded eagerly. I got the waffles out of the

freezer and stuck one in the toaster. When it was done, I popped it on a plate and put it in front of her.

"You forgot the peanut-butter-and-jelly," she said.

I sighed and opened the refrigerator. Melissa has to be the only person in the world who eats peanut-butter-and-jelly *waffles*. Usually I tease her about it and try to get her to eat them the normal way, but today I decided to live and let live.

"Here," I said, handing her the jars and a knife. "Go wild."

She put about an inch of peanut butter on and covered it with jelly. Then she picked it up and took a huge bite. She looked kind of cute — she had grape jelly smeared all around her mouth.

"Where are Patti and Lauren?" she asked after she ate her waffle.

"They went home already," I said. "Want another waffle?"

"No. Where's Stephanie?"

"At her house, I guess," I said.

Melissa squirmed in her chair. "We're supposed to go skating at the park today."

I took a deep breath. Here we go again, I thought.

"But I don't want to go," Melissa continued.

I was halfway to the refrigerator with the jar of jelly in my hand. I stopped and turned around. "What did you just say?"

"I don't want to go skating with her. I want to do something with Eileen instead."

Hurray! I wanted to yell. The days of worshipping the ground Stephanie walks on — and shops on — were over!

"Well, then, why don't you?" I said nicely instead. "If you feel like spending the day with Eileen, you should. Just call Stephanie and cancel." I didn't think Stephanie would be too upset. From the looks of things during their lip-synch performance, she had been getting a little tired of "showing Melissa the ropes" herself!

But Melissa wasn't going to be easily convinced. "You're only saying that because you don't like it when Stephanie and I do stuff together," she said. "You don't want us to be friends."

"You're the one who doesn't want to go!" I reminded her. "*I* didn't say you shouldn't. I'm just saying that if you want to do something with Eileen, you should. It isn't really nice to cancel at the last minute. But don't feel like you have to do something just because Stephanie asked you to."

Melissa was swinging her legs back and forth — she's too short for them to touch the floor. After a minute or two, she said, "I like Stephanie, but she always tells me what to do. I don't like that."

"I know!" I said. "I mean, no one likes to be told what to do . . . or what to wear, or who to be."

Melissa seemed to be thinking that over. "So it's okay if I don't like to do everything Stephanie does?"

"Sure," I said. "Stephanie is a lot older than you are." Melissa was pouting at me, so I said, "Okay, not a *lot* older — just older. She's going to want to do different things. See, your friends are your age — and my friends are my age. I mean, don't you have a lot more fun with Eileen than you do with Stephanie?"

"I guess so," Melissa admitted.

"That's because you like to do the same stuff. Just like Stephanie, Lauren, Patti, and I do." I paused for a minute. "I know sometimes you think I'm being mean when I tell you not to bug us," I said. "But you wouldn't have fun playing with us! You'd get really bored! And when you ask me to play with you sometimes, I don't want to because it would be boring for *me*. Do you understand?"

Melissa kept swinging her legs back and forth. "Does that mean we can't ever play together?" she asked.

"No, of course not!" I said. "You can do stuff with us some of the time. And you and I can go to the movies or sledding or something any time you want. You know . . . when you started hanging out with Stephanie all the time, well, it did bother me," I said slowly. "And you've been wearing red, black, and white just like Stephanie for the past two weeks!"

Melissa looked down at her red sweatshirt. "I like other colors, too," she said. "Especially blue and green!"

Like my new winter jacket. I smiled at her. "Good. Will you promise me one thing, Melissa?"

She looked skeptical. "I guess so."

"Will you throw out that Heat tape? It's really been getting on my nerves," I said.

"I can't," she replied. "I was bringing it over to Eileen's house and I dropped it and it broke," she said. "The tape got all wet, too."

I grinned. Life was finally getting back to normal at our house! "Why don't you call Stephanie now and tell her you can't go skating?" I suggested.

"Okay, I will!" Melissa jumped out of her chair and skipped over to the phone.

"After you're done, I need to talk to her, too," I said.

I listened as Melissa explained to Stephanie that she and Eileen had big plans for the day — they were going to build the biggest snow woman in Riverhurst. "Sorry!" Melissa said breezily. Then she handed me the phone. "She didn't want to go anyway," she whispered. Then she ran into the living room and I heard her asking my dad if she could borrow one of his hats.

"Hi, Stephanie," I said. "This is your wake-up call from the Beekmans."

She laughed. "Actually, I'm glad Melissa didn't want to go skating. It's too cold!"

"Are you sure about that?" I asked her. "This might be your last chance to make it big in Hollywood."

"What are you talking about?" Stephanie said.

"The movie — we have to finish it today," I said. There was something else I wanted to finish — all the bad feelings between me and Stephanie. I wanted to clear the air. "So can you come over sometime this afternoon?"

"How about three?" Stephanie said. "I have a couple of things to do first." She sounded a little uneasy about something.

"Okay," I said. "We'll all meet here at three."

"Okay," Stephanie said. "See you!"

Chapter
13

There were a few short knocks on my bedroom door. "Hi," Stephanie said shyly, walking in.

"Hi!" we all greeted her.

"Have a seat," I told her. Lauren was sitting at my desk, and Patti and I were lounging on my bed.

"Did you guys start the movie yet?" Stephanie asked.

"No, we were waiting for you," Lauren said. "I mean, we can't do anything without the whole cast! Right, Kate?"

"Right." I nodded. For some reason we were all acting weird with each other. At least Stephanie was smiling, though. She seemed like she was in a much better mood.

"So, what's the final scene going to be?" Patti asked.

"We could go back to the park and try to film

some of the boys," I offered. I knew that was what Stephanie wanted to do — I was pretty sure she wasn't planning another lip-synch routine.

"Before we do anything, I have to tell you guys what happened," Stephanie began slowly.

"You didn't get in trouble because we came over last night, did you?" Lauren asked.

Stephanie shook her head. "No. It was so great when I saw you standing outside my window. And that kit — it was terrific! I ate almost all of the brownies. The tape was hysterical. I especially liked the cards, though." Stephanie paused. "But the big thing I have to tell you is that I showed my parents that article — the one about being the oldest kid in the family."

"Really? What did they say?" Patti asked.

I sat up on the bed. "Were they mad?"

"Nope." Stephanie smiled. "I got up really early and put it on the kitchen table, like you recommended, Patti, so they'd think I just left it there by mistake."

"Then what happened?" Lauren asked.

"Well, as soon as they put the twins down for their morning nap, they came into my room and asked if we could talk. I was so nervous! But they said they were sorry if I felt like they were neglecting me. *And*, they said they'd been having a hard time adjusting to the twins, too — so it isn't just me!"

"That's funny. I don't think of parents ever having to adjust," I said. "You know what I mean? It seems like they should be used to everything already."

"Yeah, I know," said Stephanie. "I guess they have problems sometimes, too."

"I know my parents have been upset lately," Patti added. "Horace's teacher wants him to skip ahead into second grade. They're not sure if they should let him do it or not."

"So then what happened?" I asked Stephanie. "Did your parents say they'd try to do more stuff with you?"

Stephanie nodded. "They sure did. Best of all, they said they're going to hire a baby-sitter to look after the twins Tuesdays and Thursdays, so I won't have to anymore!"

"That's great!" Lauren exclaimed.

"I know! And if they need me to baby-sit, they're going to try to give me twenty-four hours' notice, instead of asking me at the last minute like they have been," Stephanie announced. "It's funny, but as soon as they said I didn't have to look after Emma and Jeremy anymore, I kind of wanted to. Isn't that weird?"

I nodded. I knew exactly what she meant. I hadn't wanted to spend any time with Melissa until someone else wanted to.

"You'll still see them all the time," Patti reminded her.

"And hear them!" Lauren added with a laugh.

"Oh, I know," said Stephanie with a wave of her hand. "But it won't be such a drag on my social life. That's another thing. When I told my parents how upset I was about missing the sleepover — I even showed them the kit — they said that my plans with you guys have top priority. So if we have a sleepover planned, they won't ask me to baby-sit, no matter what. Isn't that great?"

"Let's celebrate!" Lauren said. "I think I saw a chocolate cake downstairs on the counter."

We all jumped up and bolted downstairs. I knew it was okay for us to eat the cake — my mom had made it for us to have as a snack once we'd finished the movie. I'd helped her frost it.

I took four plates out of the cupboard. Lauren was already cutting huge slices with a knife.

"Oh, I forgot to tell you," Stephanie said. "We worked out a schedule at home so I know what my chores are and when to do them. Now I know what I have to do every day, and it's not that much. It's better than having to do whatever odd job needs doing." Stephanie took a piece of cake from Lauren.

"I agree," said Patti. "We have a schedule at my house, too. It works really well."

"Yum!" Stephanie exclaimed. "This cake is delicious."

"I should get the camera now!" I said. "You guys have cake all over your faces!"

"Well, you look like the creature from the chocolate lagoon!" Lauren reached over and wiped a glob of frosting off my cheek.

I poured four glasses of milk and passed them around. "I propose a toast," I said.

"Let me guess . . . to Kate Beekman, for her excellent directing of 'A Day in the Life of a Fifth-Grader'!" Lauren announced with a flourish.

"That wasn't what I was going to say. But I'll drink to it!" I said. We all clinked our glasses together.

"May the best film win!" Patti exclaimed.

"Oh, don't worry, it will," I said.

"With stars like us, how could it lose?" Stephanie added with a grin.

"Patti's getting a lot better," Stephanie said, coming to a stop in front of me. Lauren and Patti were skating around the rink. Lauren was still trying to go as fast as possible.

"I think Lauren's going to be an Olympic speed skater some day," I said, turning off the camcorder.

Stephanie smiled. "Remember what happened the last time we were standing here?"

"Yeah, I remember," I said.

"That was pretty funny," Stephanie said.

"I shouldn't have yelled at Melissa the way I did that afternoon," I admitted. "Though I didn't think it had been *that* funny."

Stephanie sat down on the bench beside me and started unlacing her skates.

"Actually, I've been wanting to talk to you about that," I began nervously.

"About Melissa?" Stephanie asked.

I nodded. "I'm sorry I got mad at you. I know you were only trying to be nice to her when you asked her to go shopping and curled her hair and stuff." I sketched a circle on the ice with the toe of my boot. "I guess I got mad because I felt like you were trying to take her away from me."

"The case of the stolen sister," Stephanie said with a smile. "I know. I did go kind of overboard."

"What made you want to be friends with her in the first place?" I asked.

Stephanie shrugged. "I don't know. Melissa looks up to me — to all of us. It felt nice having someone around who appreciated me."

"You mean, someone who idolized you," I said. "You don't know how many times she listened to that Heat tape, trying to get the dance right!"

"Did she really?" Stephanie shook her head. "And then I went and yelled at her when she didn't

111

do it exactly right. I guess I've been acting like a real jerk lately."

"No, not really," I said. "One good thing that came out of all this was that I noticed Melissa — as a person. I didn't know she could be so funny, or that she liked clothes, or any of that until you started hanging out with her. She was always 'Melissa the Monster,' my bratty little sister who I didn't want to be around. But when she started spending all her time with you, suddenly I wanted to be her best friend, too!"

Stephanie rested her elbows on her knees. "I guess I liked being with Melissa because she was a lot more fun to be with than the twins. Sometimes I feel like they don't even know who I am. But today, after talking to my parents, I guess I have my own family to worry about. I don't need yours, too," she said.

"Good," I said, "because Melissa is not up for adoption!"

"Do you think she'll be hurt if I don't want to hang out with her anymore?" Stephanie asked.

"Well . . . actually, I talked with her this morning, and I think she's ready to go back to doing third-grade stuff," I said.

"In other words, she'll be making your life miserable all over again?"

"Probably," I said. "But maybe I won't mind so much anymore."

Stephanie looked at me and raised one eyebrow. "Are you sure about that?"

"No," I said. "I'll probably still mind."

"Just like I'll still mind when I have to turn down my stereo or take the twins for a walk in the park," Stephanie said.

"You know what? Being an older sister is really hard." I tapped my toes against the ice. "I think we deserve some sort of medal."

"So do I," agreed Stephanie.

We both sat and stared out at the skaters for a while. Then I turned to Stephanie and said, "So is the sleepover at your house this Friday?"

"I already asked my parents and they said yes!" Stephanie said happily.

"I told you they would," I said. I love being right — especially when I don't expect to be.

Stephanie reached over and put her arm around my shoulders. "Sleepover Friends forever?" she said.

"Definitely!" I said, putting my arm around her shoulder. "And you know what, Stephanie? Some things *do* last forever!"

Chapter 14

"Aren't we going to have any popcorn?" Stephanie asked.

Everyone was over at my house for the screening of our home movie. I had dropped it off at WRIV two days ago, but no one except me had seen the final version yet. I had made a copy of it at the video store.

I was kind of nervous about how everyone would react to it. Not so much the people at WRIV — I didn't know anyone there — but my friends.

"I'll go microwave some," Lauren said.

While she was gone, I dimmed the lights and adjusted the window shades. Lauren came back a few minutes later and passed around a big bowl of popcorn, and gave everyone a glass of soda.

"Ready?" I asked everyone.

Patti and Lauren settled back onto the couch. Stephanie was lying on the floor with a pillow propped underneath her chin.

"Hit it!" Lauren yelled.

"No," Patti said, "that's *roll* it!"

"Patti's right," I said. "The correct term is 'roll it.' "

"Just start playing it already!" Stephanie said. "The suspense is killing me."

I took a deep breath and pressed the play button on the remote control. The movie opened with the title, *Fifth-Grade Funnies*.

"Hey, that's not the title we used!" Stephanie said.

"Did they mix up the movies when you got it copied?" Lauren asked me.

"No . . . ," I said.

They were all staring intently at the TV when their names came up on the screen. *Starring Stephanie Green, Lauren Hunter, and Patti Jenkins*, the poster board said.

"I don't get it," said Patti. "If we're in it, then how come — "

She didn't get to finish because the movie started. The first scene was the day I took the camera to school. There were a lot of funny shots of kids in our class eating and fooling around.

115

"This is great!" Lauren said. "Look at Henry!"

"And Taylor's in the background," Stephanie pointed out.

"Combing his hair!" Patti shrieked. "Typical!"

From that scene, the movie went straight to the shots at the park, including the one I'd taken of Stephanie watching Taylor. "Hey, I don't remember that," she said.

But Patti and Lauren started laughing.

"No fair!" Patti cried when the scene of her falling on the ice came onto the screen.

"Look at your face!" Lauren gasped.

The next shot showed Lauren in the cafeteria, stuffing half a muffin into her mouth in one bite. "Hey!" she said, startled. "You can't show this on TV!"

"Please — look at me," Stephanie said. "I look like I'm about to start bawling!" I had filmed Stephanie one afternoon when she was in a particularly bad mood. But she started laughing again when she saw her and Melissa's unsuccessful rock video.

"You look good," Patti told her.

"Yeah, right!" Stephanie howled with laughter. "Melissa's a better dancer than I am!"

"So is Noggin!" Lauren added, giggling uncontrollably.

The short interviews I had done came next. First

there was Lauren, who said her favorite thing to do after school was jog and eat. Not necessarily in that order.

"There she is — the famous actor, Lauren Hunger!" Stephanie shrieked.

"Shh — I'm next," said Patti. When I interviewed Patti, she'd been so nervous that she'd answered every question with a "yes" or a "no." I had cut all of my questions from the tape so that all you could hear was Patti saying, "Yes, no, no, no, yes, no."

"I sound like an idiot!" Patti wailed. She buried her face in a pillow.

"Here I am," Stephanie announced. Her eyes widened when she saw what part of the interview I had kept in the movie. In it, she was saying that she thought there were some things that were a lot more important than school — like shopping, and boys! "Oh no," she cringed. "I'm such an airhead!"

Then came the biggest surprise of all. I didn't think it was fair that my friends should be humiliated without me, so I had asked my father to tape me around the house a few times. There was a shot of me with my hands on my hips telling Melissa, "No, you may *not* borrow my only red-and-black sweater!" I looked like somebody's mother! My dad had also caught me coming down to the kitchen one morning — early. My hair was all clumped up on one side of my head, and I looked like a ghost — a very ugly ghost.

"Kate, you need a tan!" Stephanie cried, laughing.

"And a make-over!" Lauren said.

The film ended with a shot of the three of them with their arms wrapped around each other's shoulders, kicking their legs up in the air. And at the very end was the sign, *Directed by Kate Beekman*.

I was afraid everyone was going to be mad at me when it was over. I was prepared to run up to my room and bolt the door.

"That was great!" Stephanie exclaimed when I stopped the tape. "Play it again!"

"Did you really like it?" I asked her.

"It was the most humiliating thing I've ever seen —"

"Ten thousand times worse than my last school picture," added Patti.

"And we should probably sue you," said Lauren.

"But it was great!" Stephanie said. "How did you do it?"

"It was easy. My uncle taught me how to edit it, using the VCR and the camcorder together," I told them.

"How long did it take you?" Lauren asked.

"A long time," I admitted.

"Well, it was worth it," said Patti. "That's the funniest home movie I've ever seen!"

"We always knew you'd be a great director," Lauren said.

"Well, I could only do it because you guys were such good subjects," I said.

"Mm-hm." Stephanie nodded. "Sure."

"No, I mean it!" I said. "If you hadn't done all those silly, ridiculous things, I wouldn't have had a movie to edit!"

Lauren turned to Stephanie. "Did she just call us silly and ridiculous?"

"I think so," said Stephanie. "You know what that means."

Lauren got up and walked up behind me. "We were going to get you an Academy Award, but we didn't have enough money," she said. "So we got you this instead." The next thing I knew, she had stuck an ice cube down the back of my shirt!

"Argh!" I cried.

Just then the phone rang, and I ran into the kitchen to answer it. I was glad to escape!

"May I speak with Kate Beekman, please?" the voice on the other end of the phone said.

"This is Kate," I said. "Who's this?"

"My name is Sharon Johnson. I'm the station manager at WRIV," she said.

"Yes?" I said nervously.

"We've looked at the home video you submitted," Ms. Johnson went on. "And we all agree that it's one of the best we've seen! So we'd like to award you a special prize — Best Kids Home Movie. How does that sound?"

"Uh . . . uh . . ." I felt so stupid — I couldn't think of anything to say! I'd never really expected to win, even though I kept saying we would.

"Your video will be on our special Home Videos show next month," Ms. Johnson said. "And in addition, there's a prize of fifty dollars, and some other things that stores have donated, like a free pizza from the Pizza Palace. Congratulations!"

"Thanks," I said. I was starting to get excited. Fifty dollars! "That sounds great," I told her. "What do I have to do?"

"Just come down to the station sometime this week," Ms. Johnson said. "And ask for me. I'm looking forward to meeting you, Kate!"

"Okay," I said. "Thanks for calling." I hung up the phone and wandered back into the living room in a daze.

"Who was that?" asked Lauren.

"It better not have been my mother," Stephanie said, looking concerned.

I shook my head. "It was the TV station," I said, still unable to believe it myself.

"You're kidding! What did they say?" Lauren demanded.

"We won! It's going to be on TV next month," I said. "And we won fifty dollars and a free pizza!"

"Wow!" Stephanie jumped up from the floor and started dancing around. "We're going to be on TV!"

"Looking like idiots!" Lauren added.

"Who cares," said Patti. "We're going to be celebrities!"

Stephanie grabbed my arm and started dancing me around the room. "All right, Kate!" she said.

I looked at her and felt a big smile spread across my face. I had done it! I had made my first movie — and it was a success!

No, *we* had done it, I reminded myself. "Thanks, you guys!" I yelled. "I couldn't have done it without you!"

"We know that," said Lauren, winking at me.

Then we all sat down to watch the movie again.

Sleepover Friends forever!

#31 Lauren's Afterschool Job

We trailed Ginger past Lauren's turnoff on Brio Drive, and still Ginger kept going, past Lenox Road, Birchwood Circle, and Eagle Lane.

By now, I was definitely getting tired of playing detective. I was just going to say so to Lauren when Ginger made a sharp left turn. I was so surprised that I almost tipped over! Lauren was, too.

"Ginger's turning onto Mill Road!" she cried, screeching to a stop on the shoulder. Mill Road is Patti's street. "Come on," Lauren said.

We zoomed across Hillcrest and up Mill Road until we were almost even with the Jenkinses' driveway. Then we got off our bikes, pushed them into the hedge, and crawled in ourselves to peer out at Patti's house from between the branches.

"She's here!" Lauren said. "That's Ginger's bike beside the front steps! I can't believe it! Patti is Ginger's next victim!"